Southwold Shorts

A collection of short stories

Caroline Gay Way

Copyright © Caroline Gay Way 2019
The Coign Publishing

ISBN 978-0-244-41972-1

Other published works include:

Mindscape
Dunwich Voices
Mountain Seed
Ballad of Bladud
Stillwater by Anna Apsley (pen name)

More stories, art, poetry and video shorts can be found on
Caroline's website: carolineway.co.uk

To Venice, Simon and Southwold

Set in the Suffolk coastal town of Southwold, characters and stories have evolved from local knowledge, research and imagination. These 'Shorts' are sown together from old and new material, embroidered to enrich the towns colourful past.

Adrift in time, Southwold Shorts conflate the real and the almost real, with splashes of overlap. There is history, gentle humour, romance and the lure of long lost things. Mysteries, hints of sci-fi and slightly strange events, murders, forgotten festivals, ghosts, secrets and treasures to be found.

Contents

The Merman Sisters

Very few people remember the little mystery of the Mermaids of Southwold.

Very few people ever notice them even though they are displayed for all to see. They are almost as large as the Little Mermaid of Copenhagen, so I heard, but etched out in bas relief.

It is our memorial to the years the Merman sisters lived on Southwold's shores. A memorial from us all and the men and women they saved on that terrible night. It was my idea to depict them as mermaids 'on account of their names' as I said to the Sailors' Reading Room Committee. They all smiled remembering but there was more to it than that, as I will unfold. It's up to you what you make of it.

The sisters were both quite small to a man of my stature but they had long elegant legs that you couldn't help but notice as they walked along in fast, short stepped strides, skirts swinging to an unseen beat. Their hair was a wonder, so shiny and gold striped. It looked like spun sugar. Myrtle's short hair was sometimes styled in a finger wave shimmer as her eyes flashed from a demure downward gaze to a wide eyed 'you're amazing' glance. The way Sabrina's hair flowed down her back when she uncoiled it from her twin tortoiseshell hair combs could make a man go weak kneed at the sight of it.

Every day as the sun went down they would go for a swim in our Southwold sea. Myrtle's hair was always tucked neatly under a tight fitting swim cap. Sabrina's golden locks would flow out in waves in the breeze. Summer and winter they would walk out slowly through the cool swell until simultaneously they would dive underwater to be lost for quite some time to those who watched from the shore.

'It's healthy'! they said if people asked 'We've been to Norway and Sweden,' as if in explanation.

No one ever saw them return to their little hut called 'Splashing' on Southwold's northern shores.

Later I understood so many things. The hut by the pier, the long periods of disappearance. Now I sit on the bench in the Sailors' Reading Room garden and remember the days. The Glory Days I call them. They were like a bright flash in my life and nothing has ever matched my days with those Merman girls.

It is a Southwold story that should not be forgotten. Fact is stranger than fiction people say. Looking back I can now see how it was, but back then I was caught up in a kind of whirl. They said they loved my deep blue eyes but I'd never looked in a mirror much to know it. Myrtle's eyes were green with flecks of brown and gold. Sabrina's were also green but deep as a calm winter sea. They would hook their arms either side of me as we walked down to the shore.

They were wonderful singers too. My fingers are too stiff these days to tinkle the Joanna — but back then? Well it was a case of give me a tune and I'll play it. I just had an ear for it. Gran had an old organ in her little house in Dunwich Road when I were a nipper and that's how I learnt from the tunes on the wireless. There was a piano in the Sailing Clubhouse in those days. So I would play and they would sing and people would gather to listen to our racket.

No one knew where the Mermans came from and somehow none of us asked the question but we speculated over a pint. Their slight accent was impossible to define, it was as if they gurgled some of their vowels and their knowledge of fish was unsurpassed. They would tell us fishermen where the best catch would be and then their eyes would brim bright with tears for a moment as they told us. They were usually right about where to put down our nets and get a haul. Uncanny it was, quite uncanny. We undoubtedly had the best years of fishing with guidance from The Girls as we called them.

It was only after they disappeared that we began to realise just how mysterious they were. We realised that no one had the slightest clue as to where they had actually lived. When I accompanied them back late at night they always said goodbye as they stood at the entrance to an off street passage that led to several houses. I never got invited in. They were, shall we say, elusive but lots of fun. I never saw them dance though and it wasn't for the lack of partners vying for their attention. Three years they'd been in Southwold making our little seaside town colourful and lively as they chatted to each other in their strange unknown language. They would walk down the high street getting little keepsakes for their friends and emerging from shops with the latest London fashions in bags.

Rupert and Daphne Midgley at the museum loved the Mermans. The sisters were always popping in with their 'little finds' for the museum collection. Some were worth a fortune and got grainily pictured in the local rag.

'We love diving for treasure' they would laugh. The Amber Shop also benefitted from their sharp eyed finds as they took their early morning walks towards Benacre. They were probably making a small fortune in selling amber, but no one ever asked them directly. They were generous and witty and wonderfully adept at fielding any questions that got too close to their personal lives.

It was the night of the Great Storm, when a ship got caught up on the old stone bank, that was strangest of all for me. How many as was saved from death that night is hard to tell. The sisters brought so many that were half drowned back to shore through the crashing waves. Some of us had ropes and waded in to save the passengers and crew but the sisters were fearless and worked together saving lives. All of us fishermen were half in love with them already but after that night's work we looked on them with new eyes. But afterwards we had to ask the question — how could two such slight young women plough with such strength through the churning waves of that dread night and not be drowned?

Some London hacks came up to Southwold to cover the story but the Mermans were nowhere to be found. I kept quiet about what I had seen that night on account of not wanting to be made a laughing stock. But I know what I saw in flashes of lightening. It may have been a trick of the light but being a fisherman I know my fish and those long fish tails were like nothing I'd ever seen.

Sabrina and Myrtle came back to the Sailing Club a few weeks later when the fuss had died down, but when I caught their eye, when they first came back, I coloured up to my roots. I could feel the heat in my face. Then I could see from their eyes that they knew that I knew. We didn't have to speak of it, they knew what I had seen. We all raised a glass to their heroics on the night of the storm but I could see they were troubled and I knew it was me that troubled them.

The last time I saw them was far out to sea off Benacre. It was full moon and the sea seemed to be holding its swelling breath that night. I was just about to haul in the nets when I saw them just off the stern. They smiled and waved, but it was as if they were from another world and I somehow knew we were saying goodbye. I saw a brief flash of rainbow fish scales as they turned, diving into the depths of the sea. The haul of fish I got that night outweighed my greatest catch. A last gift perhaps.

The lawyer in the High Street called me in not long after. He said they'd given me 'Splashing' their Southwold hut and that here was the key!

That the sisters had given me 'Splashing', their hut on the north shore caused quite a stir in Southwold. None of us fishermen had ever had a visitors' hut, it was only the Black Shore huts for the likes of us to hang our nets. It was the talk of the town and caused many an unwarranted nudge and a wink. Occasionally I sit in the hut and sup a mug of tea staring out to sea and feel like a gent. Their little hut makes me a small fortune with the holiday people and I make many friends as I tell my fishy tales on the bench in the Sailors' Reading Room Garden, supping my pint from the Nelson.

But somehow nowadays I feel like I'm a fish out of water splashing around and trying to get back to the sea. Some days I feel like I will join the two of them someday soon. When the tide turns I feel it's pull.

After all Sabrina gave me a lock of her hair as a keepsake once which I've always kept in a leather pouch around my neck. So if what the old tales say is true, I could drop quietly into the waves and see them again.

I can still sometimes hear their voices singing just above the roar of the waves but my hearing is not as good as it used to be. I will always remember the shock of seeing the beauty of those rainbow scales flashing in the moonlight. I hold that memory close to my heart. What I saw may have been a trick of the light. I can no longer tell the truth of it. Often I wade into the sea and think of joining them, but I was never taught to swim.

Sleeping under the Pier

Orwell only did this on rainy nights out of a perversity of mood. He knew his mother would be agitated and his father would pace the floor before exasperated, he would go to bed muttering, 'Why — why' under his breath with every step.

George delighted in imagining the scene.

Slipping in just after dawn had broken he would roll naked into bed. This in itself was a subversive act in a resolutely pyjama wearing age.

At breakfast, which he was obliged never to miss when living under his father's roof, he would pedal his usual line of the health giving properties of the outdoor life, inculcating a hardiness of constitution advocated by the army corps. He would quote from a dogeared army manual he had picked up on one of his trips to the North.

He enjoyed seeing his father unable to argue successfully against such a seemingly healthy notion.

'Nobody else does such a thing' his father would conclude as he marched off to read *The Times*.

'George' his mother would say, in a mildly reproving way, after his father had left the room. At which point George would wink at his sister. His mother rarely made further comment.

Both George and his sister would drink tea twice a day. Even when he was a 'Gentleman of the Road' he would make sure that he had a flattened box of tea in his pocket and matches to light a fire under his billy can. He believed in the health giving properties of tea.

'The two great cities of Tokyo and London grew to such enormous size because tea keeps the gut healthy and tea leaves keep the drains clean,' he would say to fellow travellers.

His sister would sometimes regale her Southwold tearoom customers with this obscure titbit of information. They would smile politely and express amazement. Sometimes they would ask tentatively after George as they knew he had become some sort of writer.

'Has he been to Tokyo?' they would enquire.

'We had cousins who grew up in Bangalore. He had a Russian a friend whose father was in the revolution.'

'Goodness !' The ladies would exclaim 'How exotic!'

There were a great deal of 'Maiden Aunts' who lived in Southwold. These were ladies who were unable to find husbands due to the enormous amount of young men that had been killed in the trenches and the 1919 flue epidemic that carried away so many more. These ladies lived on memories, fortitude and tea. They spent their days looking after sick relatives who had been prescribed sea air by their doctors and busily organising good works for the needy.

One lady was a particularly regular customer in the tearoom. She would always glow rather pink at the mention of George. She had a particularly loquacious friend whom she had told about a somewhat romantic kiss with George under the pier. They had been forced to take shelter from a sudden squall and he had wrapped his arms around her to keep her from taking a chill.

The story had passed behind gloved hands.

When she heard the story herself, George's sister smiled and wondered just how many ladies had been caught in the same way under the shadow of Southwold pier.

George Orwell's parents moved to Southwold in 1921. His sister later opened a teashop.

15

Falling into the Sea

For Laura

There is a strangeness
about a house
that is falling
into the sea

There is a sense of displacement
a sense
of energy dispersing

Entities maybe
Perhaps...

There is a sense of the known world receding as the wild desolation of the sand road begins to unfold towards the Benacre Edge.

All along the northernmost beach of Southwold bricks lie scattered like lost souls. These sanded wave-washed broke-brick remnants are the first markers of the desolation. Indicators of breaking away from the familiar Southwold streets. Wild breakers roll into shore — breaking and biting into soft protective cliffs.

I have always lived in Southwold. Always been in this house. There were five more houses nearer the sea, so long ago, I can only just remember. I had learned to count to five, which mother had taught me, walking along past them towards the beach.

The house that went into the sea one night made boyhood learning of subtraction a very real thing. I understood subtraction after that night. The wind was blowing a gale. Mrs Avering ran to our house in her nightie with her hair in a plait down her back. Her man had gone into the sea with the house 'cos he went back to save stuff. He was never seen again. I was sitting on the stairs watching her cry, listening to the wind howling and shaking the windows.

Derelict houses make great dens. I have found treasures and truths about lives in forgotten journals.

I walk along the beach every day. The broken things attract me. The beach holds many broken things. Screams and cries get lost in the enfolded curl of waves. I hear lost cries. Few know that gulls are imitative birds.

Time has unfolded down the years in tidal waves.

As a boy I got into the paper for finding a gold watch.

I never got that lucky again but it gave me a taste for looking. Jackdaw they used to call me and that was as good a name as any an' I stuck to it. Ma had gone years back, she never did come back one Wednesday. Never did find out what happened. Dad crossed over one night after boozing on one of his sad nights. He liked taking off his belt to me when he got back.

'He was falling down drunk most nights, must have hit his head,' I told Hebditch our town Bobby. Said he had probably hit it on one of those house bricks on the beach and got pulled out in the rip tide. It was days before he washed up. I've still got that brick somewhere.

So many secrets I found when he had gone. A whole box under the bed and other stuff. Small papers stacked with peculiar diagrams. Something like the stuff that's in our shed. Strange writing, it was no language I'd ever seen, looked more like code.

I keep hearing mother in my head — she calls me but I can't come. I don't know where she is. She told me she was a mermaid once. You could believe it was true the way her hair was so long. She said the plaster picture on the wall outside the Southwold Sailors' Reading Room was of her and her sister, done by my dad in his younger days, when they first met. Dad was an artist of sorts. Mum liked to tell stories. She told me stories about the broken things we found on the beach. Wonderful tales they were. I try to remember some and some I try to forget. I find more and more broken bits of lives washed up — salt scoured and cleaned by the relentlessness of waves.

I swim every day of the year. On the edge of my mind I look for Mum in the waves. Dad said she'd gone to see her sister for a long visit. But years passed and she never came back. She never told me she was going away. I used to go to the wardrobe to smell her clothes. Then one day they were gone.

'Get out of there you little alien,' he'd say when he found me sleeping there, but it was where I felt closest to Mum. Her wardrobe was the only thing left of her in the house.

He made sure I was strong, my father did. He would chase me into the waves for swimming every day of the year. We would walk for miles searching for lost things.

I walk up all along to Benacre and Covehithe every day looking for signs. He told me his ship had crashed. We found some debris in the broken bits washed up and kept them in the shining shed.

On Moon Nights I've shore fished for more years than I can count, scanning the skies like father used to do. His name for stars was different from the books I've seen. His word for comets was just a sound. It sounded like a train heard far away.

He told me once, when he was in his cups, he was waiting for a ship — waiting to be taken back somewhere.

'Over the sea to sky' he'd sing quite softly. Just that line over and over as he looked up at the clouds.

I feel somehow that I am waiting still.

SouthWorld Secret Seven

This is a story about a book of stories that Carrie wrote about SouthWorld. A book begun by Carrie when she was seven and three-quarters, with her first pictures of the SouthWorld Kingdoms. She started her first map when she was nearly eight and a quarter.

Every year Carrie's family came to SouthWorld for their holidays. Her great grandfather and grand mother had been in something called the Raj. Carrie thought it was some sort of secret society and was something to do with living in India and then coming back. Her dad made what he called 'Raj Curry' sometimes from grandmother's old recipe notebook.

Anyway it meant holidays by the sea when the house wasn't let out. Carrie had had dresses let out as she grew bigger. Mummy had to let out the seams. So Carrie sometimes played with the sewing machine peddle to make the needle go up and down faster and faster and wondered how they did that for houses. She could see some places in the walls of the old house that looked a bit like seams in the plasterwork. She thought, when she was small, that that was where the house had been let out.

Written and drawn in a secret note book she had bought on the Pier, Carrie's SouthWorld had Seven Kingdoms.

There was *The Domain of Dune* which she loved the best. She loved playing roly-poly down the little hills and making little nests. Constructing driftwood hideouts or running along *The Royal Path* between the dunes. She wrote stories about the *Noble Dogs* who led their people along the SouthWorld paths and pavements and the *Little Sand People* who got

21

children to build their summer homes each day before the tide.

The Town Territory had alleyways for exploration. Carrie loved looking at the gardens over the walls, especially if they had wild rabbits. There were several sweet shops in the town and some of the houses had 'sort of' towers. Every year there was at least one new tower to find. Carrie wrote about the *Rapunzel People* whose hair grew long in Southwold — hair they let down in dead of night. When she spotted a lady with her hair up she wondered if they had a tower.

There was the *The High Common Land* which had lots of paths and secret nooks where she would spend hours exploring and mapping. There was treasure to be found there sometimes, when golf balls were discovered and sold back to golfers — or the golf club, which was very grand. *The High Common Land* was breathtaking at sunset when it became a theatre of coloured light and Carrie would stand watching it in sheer delight after supper. It was a show that was on almost every night without an audience except for Carrie. Carrie wrote about the *High Common People* who were mostly invisible.

The Marsh Land Kingdom was the province of majestic swans and strangely magical looking cream coloured cows.It had a strange bleak atmosphere. It was a lost land of birds and raised paths and Carrie was convinced it was inhabited by *Marsh-Wiggles* if only she could find them. Carrie filled a whole book about the further adventures of *Marsh-Wiggles*.

Warblers Witch Territory was across the foot bridge or a trip in the little ferry row boat. Carrie explored several long summers looking for the Warblers' Witch whom she hoped

22

could cure the wart on her hand. Mummy said that it wasn't very noticeable. But Carrie was embarrassed and conscious of it when anyone tried to hold her hand in a circle game.

The Pier Dominion had noisy fun and crazy mirrors. The only food people ate there was ice cream and chips. The Pier Dominion included the *Bright Huttish Settlements* all along the seafront. Carrie mused on what the 'seaback' might look like. A look behind the scenes in a theatre with bits of dry seaweed hanging up, perhaps? She had seen this strange back theatre world when she had played a scene from *Alice Through the Looking Glass* for the Summer Theatre Talent Contest at St Edmonds Hall, but the '*Bless This House*' boy won.

The Harbour Territory was where the family sometimes had a tea treat in the big windowed *Chocolate-Cake Place* looking out at the boats. Also 'fish-on-fat' chips on a bench by the water was fun because they could eat with their fingers. Carrie loved the step-down, step-up pub with its big flood ruler. Carrie drew pictures and wrote about mermaids and mermen having their drinks under water. This was when it became the *In The Drink* bar. Sometimes from there she ran to explore over the *Water Bridge* and wave across to her family from the path opposite.

There was also the mysterious Black Shore Huttish Settlement, as well as the Huttish Settlements in the *Wablers Witch Territory*. The huts Carrie liked the best were hidden behind the dunes. Carrie wrote a long story about living there.

Carrie found the Warblers' Witch lady she was looking for one August over in the furthest Huttish Settlement. She had been walking the sea edge and decided to visit the magic circle of black huts. One had a smoking chimney and a lady was sitting in a rocking chair in the evening sun. A black cat was sitting on her lap, so Carrie thought this could be the right sort of sign. Carrie asked her the name of the cat and the lady answered that only cats knew their names, so of course Carrie knew she was 'One'. She told her about the wart and the Magic Lady passed her hands slowly over Carries hand for a few minutes.

'It'll be gone in a week,' she said.

'Thank you,' said Carrie as waved her goodbye.

As it was raining Carrie decided to make new maps of each of the territories scorch the edges and tie them into scrolls with ribbons. It took her a long time, several days in fact. When the sun came out again she went for a walk around by the town light house. She was thinking about creating a map of the streets from there to the Summer Theatre.

After a while a boy rode alongside her on a bike. Carrie pretended not to notice him.

'Where is your note book? You always have a notebook!'

Carrie gave the boy a sideways glance. He looked cool.

'Not always' she answered with a glancing smile. She was glad the wart on her hand was gone at last. Carrie smiled at him and he smiled back. Carrie then decided she might have a new kingdom to explore.

Northwold Lost

A few miles south of Southwold is Dunwich but almost no-one remembers the little fishing village of Northwold which was lost to the sea in the early part of the 20th century.

It lay between Easton Bavents and Covehithe. If you look at the map three coastal bites can be seen between Orford and Kessingland. One includes the increasingly well known story of Dunwich, the city that drowned. The second bite does not include any settlements but it is the story of the drowned village of Northwold that is perhaps, in its own way, just as interesting as the story of Dunwich. Although it's inundation was rather more recent.

There is very little documented evidence about swimming in the early part of the 20th century. However what took place in the Victorian era, in terms of swimming, is quite fascinating.

There was the Flying Gull, a native American Indian who shocked the refined British public by winning a swimming competition in London with his frantic crawl technique. This swimming method was previously unknown to these shores. He settled in Northwold for some time before returning to America and taught them all his crawl technique to power through the waves.

So Northwold, in its day became rather unexpectedly, the swimming capital of Britain. Its popularity had much to do with it's shallow waters that provided resting points like stepping stones that stretched far out to sea. This was the remains of a great stone bank. It's shallowness provided some swimmers with the possibility of reaching the far horizon.

The Flying Gull heard tell of the little coastal village where all the inhabitants swam. He decided to track down this village as it reminded him of the tale his Native American ancestors told about the time before they were forced to lived on reservation land. Tales of a far off time when they lived by the sea. His visit was written up by a London paper and caused a bit of an influx of Victorian men in striped swimsuits to Northwold and Southwold for some time.

People can still occasionally be seen standing on the underwater remnants of the old Kingsholm bank at Southwold, that once reached to Dunwich before it was breached. At Northwold there were a series of offshore stone banks reaching far out to sea. They are the remnants of Doggerland, but that's another story.

Both the men and women that lived in Northwold took up the swim challenge every year. It was a village tradition little known outside the immediate vicinity. The whole village would swim out to the first ridge. Then the men and some of the women would swim to the second ridge further out. The tradition was that they waved back to the others and some then went on further out to the furthest ridges. Some of them swam every day of the year which made them hardy and long lived. The oldest inhabitants, it was said, lived to be over 100 years old.

It was this unusual village pastime that saved them when the inundation came. That and the fact that their old tarred boats were often used upturned as roofs for their pinch thin houses stuffed with rags to keep out the worst of the cold east wind.

The Flying Gull and Tobacco
by George Catlin 1844

The villagers of Northwold were mostly resettled in Southwold after their homes were swept away and to this day some high cheek boned individuals can be spotted in the old Sailors' Reading Room photos. These features can also be found in a few native Southwoldians. It is rumoured they may be descendants of the Flying Gull who had stayed for some years in Northwold on and off. There were several shy young men who got lucky with marrying pretty girls during those years. The Flying Gull was not a marrying man and would swim away down the coast for a while, when there was trouble, but would always return. Until one day he did not. The rumour was he had had decided to swim back to America.

Northwold was a close community and looked after its own even though some of the first born did not take after their fathers. It enhanced their swimming stock to have a famous swimmer in their mix. And even now there are those take the plunge every single morning from Southwold beach. If you get up early enough to see them take the plunge. Some of them may be descendants of the Flying Gull. If they have high cheekbones and black hair it is possible they are descended from those that lived in the swimming village of Northwold.

Flying Gull is a real historical person who is said to have brought a new kind of swimming to England.

Apparently no-one has ever heard of Northwold!

1922 Bob

For Jane Bennett

I have a little piece of Southwold that is about two metres square.

It has been in my family since my flapper Aunt B cut her hair into a bob around 1922. I know this because there was an enormous family row about it that chuntered on down the years. An ongoing family row that started with the hairstyle and the hut! Perhaps she was the first woman to buy her own Southwold hut. She was probably the first young woman to cut her hair and outrage the rather proper ladies of Southwold. Who knows? But the family did not approve.

I knew about it growing up because my grandfather and my father ranted on, in an exasperated way, whenever they talked about her.

Mother and I have never cut our hair, we never even considered it. Father ruled us with a rod of iron. From the snippets I pieced together about my great aunt over the years I gathered she had never married. The family did not approve of this lack of enthusiasm for marriage.

So I don't think I saw the hut when I was growing up or if I did I was too young to remember. There is a faded snapshot of me as a toddler on a beach, which may or may not have been taken at Southwold.

After 'B' died my father sold her house and rented out the hut for extra income. We had not, as far as I could remember, ever visited but when I inherited it I got curious and went to see it. It looked rather forlorn, with its cracked peeling paint, old vinyl floor covering and down-at-heel camping chairs. I did not stay long.

I got a phone call from the chippy I had hired to refurbish — did I know there was a trap door in the floor? Did I still want the vinyl replaced? To my surprise he also asked if I had the key.

'What key?' I asked. 'Have you lost the one I gave you?'

'No' he replied in his delightful Suffolk tones 'Tis a key to the trap door you'll be wanting, if you got one. Or shall I just put down the new vinyl over it like we agreed?'

'No leave it for a few days, there was an odd key with the papers. I'll look for it and come down next weekend. Just lock up for now and let me have the bill for what I owe you to date.'

My great-aunt B had been an archaeologist out in Egypt and the Middle East. I hadn't realised she was quite so famous in the archaeology world until I looked her up in an old book she had written on Petra. I also found some interesting entries about my aunt 'B' and Vita Sackville-West in some old diaries. The wags of the time used to rib them by saying 'Hello Bob!' as they walked around in their boyish jackets. How sweetly outrageous they looked in the old photo I found of 'B' and Vita.

The trapdoor continued to intrigue me throughout some busy weeks in the fashion trade in Town. Finally the work subsided and the late September sunshine called me from London towards the coast and a breath of fresh air. I motored up in Dad's old Morgan and drew into the courtyard of the Swan in less than three hours. In the silence, after I had turned off the engine, a seagull squawked a raucous welcome. My bags were soon stowed away in my room, which was a little stuffy, so I strolled towards the sea looking for a tea shop. The sea air was wonderfully fresh after the summer dust of London.

I had found the key in a folded brown envelope in the lawyer's papers. Tied to it was an old brown luggage label. The writing on the label was small, faded and spidery. I couldn't make out what it said and thought I might try to decipher it after I had opened the trap door, if it wasn't completely jammed after so many years of seaside weather. Perhaps a magnifying glass would prove useful as I was becoming a bit of a sleuth into Aunt B's affairs!

Some Southwold huts get moved into the car park over the winter and some are fixed. B's was a static one set in front of a low cliff bank near the old town.

Walking along in the cool breeze and sunshine I thought about the enigmatic poem someone had written to her in a book on her Egyptian expeditions that I had found in the London Library.

The trapdoor certainly seemed a rather an odd thing to find in the floor of a Southwold hut. But maybe many of the huts had them for all I knew. Perhaps they had been used to store fishing nets or something.

Closing the double doors of the hut behind me I knelt down. My curiosity level was now quite high. The keyhole looked mysteriously old. Would it need some oil to turn it I wondered?

I found it seemingly impossible to turn the key but just as I was about to give up the key clicked and I was able to lift the door in the floor.

I don't know what I expected but brick steps and a bulbous old fashioned light switch were rather surprising. The brickwork was somehow so substantial compared to the flimsiness of the wooden hut. Flipping on the light switch quite gingerly in case of old wiring, I found that it still actually worked. I descended the short flight of stairs to a small arched tunnel that was adorned with Egyptian text and pictures. The colours were so extraordinarily vivid, I actually gasped. The sound echoed into the shadowed distance. I looked back to the square of daylight at the top of the steps, then turned to explore the extraordinary tunnel. After some distance the tunnel began to curve, around the corner the floor began a gentle incline towards the ceiling.

I was beginning to feel quite claustrophobic. I was also beginning to wish I had not been quite so spontaneously inquisitive. What if these old fashioned lights suddenly went out and I was left in the dark. In a very few steps the musty smelling tunnel led to a dead end with a wall that was covered from floor to ceiling with more brightly coloured Egyptian hieroglyphs and an Egyptian queen. Looking up I saw a wooden handle above my head. I just couldn't stop myself. Without thinking I just reached up and pulled it.

'Good afternoon!' A head appeared. 'Would you like a hand up? You seem to have taken my hearthstone!'

'How…?'

'I heard your footsteps as you came along!' An elegant male hand reached to help me up.

A little later I stood in a spacious drawing room overlooking Gun Hill while the old gentleman, who had introduced himself as Ernest, got me a 'spot of tea'. Over the mantle piece was a large picture of Vita West and my Aunt B having tea in her amusingly named *Tut Hut.*

'I painted that, you know' said the old man in rose coloured corduroy trousers from Denny's, as he appeared with a tea-tray.

'We were the Three Musketeers. Vita was a damn good shot!'

'I was their very own, very young man — I was quite the baby of our little trio.'

'I bat for the other side you know, so I was their safe escort in town and a consort in their trials and tribulations. Looking at you quite takes me back. You look so like her — you simply must be B's great niece…'

'Charlotte,' I smiled and took a sip of Earl Grey.

'I am afraid I didn't know her at all. There was a family row. My grandfather and father… I think there was some sort of scandal.'

'Well I am afraid I was the scandal! We both were — myself and Vita. The scandal was because all of us lived here together in B's house. *Menage a trois* we called it. So it was rather racy — not to our Chelsea Arts crowd of course, but here in Southwold it certainly raised a few eyebrows. You came here once when you were very small, I had a small box camera and took a snapshot of you.'

'Yes I've seen it. B must have sent it to my parents.'

'She did. It was a little peace offering after yet another family row. Your father found our domestic arrangements quite unacceptable. I remember your grandfather being quite outraged when, arm in arm, the three of us bumped into him one night coming out of his club in Pall Mall!'

'I bet that was..... interesting'

'Quite.......' Ernest laughed to himself and offered me a little biscuit.

For some moments he appeared lost in his memories as he stared at the rectangular darkness where his hearthstone used to be.

'So you know about the tunnel?' It's quite beautiful. Have you really never seen it?'

'B mentioned something about it in a joking sort of way, I never took it seriously. I think she brought Carter down for a little stay. She knew him quite well I think, but I never met him. I got the impression they may have fallen out later on. So I believe Carter helped her with some of the spade work. Well, being archaeologists they both knew how to dig! I remember her laughing and saying it started out as a small project.

I believe she sealed the tunnel up years ago.'

'But why?' I looked at him, hoping he could give me an answer.

'Why on earth did she build it. It seems such an odd thing to do'.

For the first time he looked a little thrown — a little off balance.

'I got the impression from B it was something to do with Tut's treasure. Tutankhamun and all that. Maybe it was a store house of sorts.'

'You mean stuff from the Valley of the Kings ?'

'I think so. A bit hush hush and probably under the radar so to speak.'

He winked at me! Nobody had done that in years.

'Southwold does have a small harbour you know!'

I gave a low whistle. So that was a turn up for the books. My aunt might have been involved in somewhat shady dealings.

I knew there was a family history that she had found a gold hoard in Jordan and mother had once reminded father that she had also reputedly found the site of the Garden of Eden. Father snorted with derision.

I stirred my tea thoughtfully and looked up at the painting of the two elegant young women, one in a bathing suit and swimming cap and one in a sailor top and Coco Channel trousers. My aunt had clearly acquired some measure of fortune in her own right.

I decided to change the subject.

'Do you know why she was called B? I've always been curious about that'

'Oh that? That was the Bob!' 'The Bob?' I looked up at him quizzically.

'I believe your Aunt B was the first woman in England to chop off her hair into a boyish bob! I think they were on the sherbet. They got completely smashed one night! Your Aunt B just loved to be outrageous and Vita got out the scissors! Bob was the boy who delivered the papers! They thought it was terribly funny to call B's short hairstyle a bob. Then a fashion magazine featured B's new style and... well the bob became all the rage.

*   *   *   *

'But of course there is the other thing about 1922. It was later that year that B went on Carter's dig in Egypt'. That's partly why she cut her hair — the heat you know, that and the fact that she could pass for a young man and get more respect from the natives. She looked rather splendid in her long boots and jodhpurs if the picture is anything to go by and she did have quite a determined chin — not unlike your own if I may say so,' he added with a little smile and a wink. When, I wondered, did winking go out of fashion.

'She had been out there with Carter before but that was the year of their great find.'

'They found it together?'

'Well that's the way B tells it. Of course Carter was the senior man and had every right to claim the prize for himself but I believed B when she said that she did the spade work — the research that led them to the hidden tomb.

'Would you like to see her room?'

He lent forward his eyes full of boyish enthusiasm.

'I kept it just as she had it all those years ago — nothing has been changed'

'So it was you who bought the house from my father!'

I had to admit this was rather a surprise.

'Yes. A little subterfuge was needed on my part. I don't think he would have sold it to me had he known who was really buying it. Although, that being said, I don't think he actually knew my real name even though we had met on occasion. Vita and Bob always referred to me as *Boyzy* — better than some of the other nicknames I got at school'

'How amazing to have kept her room unchanged all these years.'

'Yes, well well it has been rather a while, so it maybe a little dusty. Actually I couldn't bear to go in. It holds such memories for me of the fun we had. I would wake them with a little tea. Anyway you would be welcome to use the room if you would like to but we'd have to get out the vacuum cleaner. At the very least you could go and have a look and a have little rummage.

Everything in it belongs to you' I have been hoping you would turn up one day. You might even unearth some of her secrets. I always knew she had secrets. That was part of the fun.'

I stared at him wide-eyed and curious.

'You mean I can go up there right now?'

'Do. Do. Take your time then come down and tell me what you think and what you've found. Everything there is yours. She was your aunt after all. It's through the double doors at the top of the stairs I haven't opened it for years. So mind the spiders'

'I don't mind spiders. Have you ever read Charlotte's Web?'

I giggled slightly as I felt my spirits rise. It was turning out to be quite an afternoon. This was something like a childhood adventure and I didn't need to be asked twice.

Ernest pointed through the archway to the wide stairs beyond.

'Enjoy!' He said, waving me onwards and chortling to himself. I don't think he had had such fun in years.

The double doors proved to be a bit stiff but I rattled them back-and-forth until they opened. A shaft of afternoon light spread like a spotlight from the top of the tall window. The huge room looked like a 1920s film set — somewhat out of focus, as only long deserted dusty rooms can be.

It took me a while to understand what I was seeing. One of the largest beds I had ever seen faced the window. I gasped in surprise as I saw there were two figures standing in the corner of the room in strange costumes. Behind them was a huge swathe of floor-to-ceiling material painted like a large cityscape of a mediaeval Russian town. I had seen this somewhere before but I couldn't at first recall where. Then it came to me — *The Rite of Spring*!

I had seen it in an exhibition at the Victoria and Albert Museum it was a stage backdrop.

On the table beside costumes was a windup gramophone with a great trumpet speaker and a stack of 78 records in their brown paper sleeves. No doubt I would find Stravinsky's music amongst them. A large jug adorned the dresser. I wiped a little dust off it with my sleeve and saw two abstracted faces, it was undoubtedly a Picasso. Perhaps the two faces were Vita and Aunt B.

I opened the huge art deco wardrobe and saw a feast of 1920s and 30s fashion, several mothballs rolled out across the floor.

I peered out of the window. Southwold lay below me, beyond that was the sea. My head was spinning. So this was my legacy. A legacy from an aunt I never knew. No wonder the world of fashion had attracted me. It was obviously a genetic trait.

But there was nothing I could see as yet of Egyptian origin. However the light was going and there would be plenty of time to examine the room's contents another day.

* * * *

'Would you like a little pink gin or are you a cocktail girl?'

'Well yes I feel like I need one. There are some amazing treasures in that room. Pink gin please.'

'Well I expect you've only scratched the surface of what's up there. B told me that room held a special secret but she never told me what it was. You will have to set about finding some treasures.'

'But this is your house surely everything in it belongs to you'

'In a way that's true but I bought the house because of my friendship with B. I always hoped you'd come and find me one day. It seemed a kind of sacrilege to do anything with B's room. So I left it as it always was. I bought the house contents and all.'

'The costumes from *The Rite of Spring* gave me a bit of a turn I thought they were real people for a moment or ghosts'

'I had quite forgotten those costumed mannequins. That was a marvellous night. I was in it you know and so, in a way, were they.'

'Who Vita and B?

'That's where they met. It was Vita's 21st birthday present — to go to *The Rite of Spring.* All London was buzzing with rumours about it. That was her big coming out party treat. Dear B was sweet 17.

They met in the powder room, they were both wearing outrageous long evening trousers which was highly avant-garde and quite frowned upon in those days. They burst out laughing and decided to sashay down the stairs into foyer together. Well, they hit it off immediately. Vita introduced B to her people. After *The Rite* performance, which was rather a shambles in some ways but incredibly exciting as well, they partied all night. The rest is history.

'So how did you know Vita? How come you were actually in *The Rite of Spring*?'

'It was completely extraordinary. A life changing event — talent spotted in a school play. Swept up to London in a Daimler with my housemaster's wife as a chaperone as I was rather young. The *Ballets Russes* needed an extra boy as their Russian lad got had scarlet fever. My pater knew the Sackville-Wests, so I was their house guest for a while in their London pad. Vita took me under her wing when she came up to town.

Come back in the morning and will have another chat over coffee'

This story was inspired by Crystal Bennett, an archaeologist relative whom I loved and greatly admired.

SandWitches on Southwold Beach

For my sister

The two little ladies had been concocting it since early morning.

Lady Caroline had awoken with a revelation. She loved Scandal! Somehow she wanted to create something that would be an expression of this new found feeling of love and appreciation that had engendered such warm feelings as the early dawn light filtered though the curtains. It was a particularly bright fresh light full of the exciting squealing, peeling, laughter of gulls.

What had Daddy called this place last night when they had arrived so late — 'SouthWorld' or 'SouthMould' or something. Anyway a south place by the sea. They had seen the waves by the street lamps as they drove along.

Lady Caroline had woken early, no one else was up and Scandal was scraping and pawing at the door as she came down the stairs. She opened the kitchen door quietly and slid herself in without letting Scandal out and waking the whole house. Scandal gave a little whine of greeting and for the first time she could ever remember she hugged the spaniel with a squeeze of heartfelt affection. Scandal wagged his tail even harder.

Lady Caroline saw that Scandal's dog bowl was empty and began filling it with some interesting liquids and powders she found under the sink. A little of this. A squeeze of that. A few drops of something else. All for Scandal who she now knew she loved.

Scandal looked interested at first because he knew his bowl was being filled with something and he wagged his tail. As the smells in his bowl were definitely not right he lost interest and lay in his dog bed looking bored and a bit sad.

Every now and then Lady Caroline would pull him across the kitchen floor towards her lovely concoction, made with her new strong love, and tried to get him to show an interest.

He didn't seem very glad about it, so she tried really hard to find other bright and smelly things at the back of the under sink cupboard to add to some dog biscuit to encourage him. She was quite certain in her mind that at some point she would get it just right and Scandal would love it and lick his bowl clean. It had such interesting colours and smells.

Lady Caroline just knew how Scandal loved smells. He was always pulling on his lead to find smells. He even tried to smell up ladies' skirts which was quite rude of him she thought. It was quite plain to Lady C that he could smell flies and bees because his nose would follow their every move. She had, though she had tried to look away, seen him curl himself round to smell under his own tail. So she knew if she could get the mixture really smelly Scandal would just love it.

Lady Josephine joined her after a while and suggested salt and pepper from the table top and soap flakes to make it thicker might also help. But Scandal could not be persuaded to try it and dug his paws in even though they got his nose quite close to the special concoction. The little ladies were rather put out by this time because they had tried really hard to show Scandal how much they loved him and he didn't seem interested in the strong smelly mix in his bowl.

Neither was Daddy when they showed him proudly what they had made and were so disappointed when he threw it away and poor Scandal had to have boring water and biscuits.

Lady Caroline had eaten ordinary sandwiches with paste and jam at parties. But Daddy had told her there were definitely going to have 'SandWishes' on Southwold beach. The idea of SandWishes on the beach seemed magical to Lady Caroline. She couldn't wait to get to the sandy shore to start making them. She would stir sand and sea water in her tin bucket and be a Sand Witch making spells. Daddy had said that holidays were magic in the car driving down.

She knew that there were Sand Fairies who granted wishes if she could find one. And she knew she had a really important wish. She decided a magic sand potion would do the trick, so she set about creating a sand mixture to attract the Sand Wish Fairy to her part of the beach. By the end of the week Lady Caroline had tried every different kind of sand mixture and making sand fairy rings with no success.

Lady Josephine seemed more interested in paddling, making sand castles, and watching birds but on Friday she let Lady Caroline use some drops from her tiny bottle of Woolworth scent in her latest SandWish mixture, on the understanding that if Lady Caroline found a Sand Fairy, Lady Josephine would get a wish as well.

Lady Caroline knew exactly the wish she would make if she could find the Sand Fairy and make a SandWish. She stretched her eyes as far as they would go in her increasingly anxious search for a Sand Wish Fairy on SouthWorld beach.

Lady Caroline had a sudden inspiration. Perhaps Scandal could find the Sand Fairy. He was always running off and searching for things. She called him over. She petted him, telling him with every stroke that she hadn't forgotten the morning she had loved him so much. She told him silently that her mind had been filled with other thoughts.

She lifted her latest sand and scent concoction to Scandal's nose, she was sure this one really was magic with the extra drops of scent. She lifted up his long floppy ear and whispered to him gently. He sat patiently, his tail making little furrows in the sand. Then he lifted his damp brown nose and started to run towards the dunes.

Caroline watched Scandal intently as he ran towards the dunes. Could he? Would he find the Sand Fairy? Would she get her dearest wish granted? Her heart fluttered with longing. Scandal disappeared. After a minute or two she stood up very straight and took a few steps towards the dunes, and made her wish.

'Don't go too far, little lady' called Uncle Micheal from the picnic rug.

Suddenly Caroline began to smile.

Scandal emerged and was circling a sand mound they had dug and decorated with stones near the dunes.

'He must have found the Sand Fairy!'

Uncle Micheal looked puzzled.

Caroline pointed. 'Look Uncle Mike, look!'

Over the sand dunes Mummy was coming. Scandal was jumping up all around her.

Jo looked up and started running up the beach.

Caroline stood quite still feeling the magic of the moment. She had not seen her mother since before the holidays. Her dearest wish had happened and Mummy was here at last, and she knew she would always love Scandal for finding the invisible Sand Fairy that had granted her important Sand Wish on SouthWorld beach.

Caroline started running her heart bursting with happiness.

Daddy and Auntie Joan appeared behind Mummy and gave Uncle Michael a wave.

'I think it's time we took our two "little ladies" for some ice cream.' He called, 'They've been waiting a long time.'

Caroline jumped up into her mothers arms and knew she was the luckiest girl in the whole wide world.

The Southwold Towers Mystery

There are several houses in Southwold that have small towers set high up in the roof. But there is only one house in which something out of the ordinary occurred.

If you see someone looking up, walking slowly past such a house, it may be that they are one of the few that know the true location. They might be a person who actually knows something about what happened or has heard rumours.

It may be that they are Southwold residents trying to guess. Some think they know more than most people as to the actual location and circumstance. If you ask them, I doubt if they will tell you anything. Mostly Southwold likes to keep its' secrets. They will see that you are burning to know and you might offer to buy them a coffee and some might accept. If you should get that lucky, you may indeed learn a great deal about Southwold's underbelly if they are residents, but chances are that they too are secret mystery hunters and know very little more than you do yourself.

If you are interested in The Southwold Mystery you will, of course have read *The Omni House* and *Branes Old Tales*. and will have noted down some of the secreted clues. Like many you will have become intrigued enough to come to Southwold to see for yourself if you can throw more light on the events that took place there and find the turret house where it all occurred.

There are two houses that seem, from the evidence, more likely than the others. However divulging why this might be so, would spoil what after all is a wonderful mystery that has brought people to Southwold for many years. It has meant, over time, that every back street or High Street house above street level, has been viewed from all possible angles and photos taken.

Some people, after reviewing the facts and returning on various occasions and seasons, take the view that there may be a portal key to be found. This may be why we have so many metal detector hunters attracted to the town, slowly scanning the beaches.

But others, as in *Marne's Table of Amendments*, believe the portal key, that may or may not exist, is not an actual key, but is in fact an artefact with some ancient design that will fit or match something when the real turret is finally found. This will then lead on to the final phase and the whole mysterious event will be cleared up and brought finally into the light.

When this occurs it is highly likely that the hundreds and thousands of people that have become interested and even obsessed with the mystery over the years will come flocking to Southwold's 'almost island'. There will undoubtably be traffic problems with only one entrance to the town. Few that have searched the town for clues over the years will want to miss out on being in Southwold in person to see for themselves how the mystery unfolds.

Some will feel a sense of relief that the mysterious events have at last been found to have a rational explanation. Some may feel that, even so, there is more to it than can be properly explained away by diagrams and dotted lines or news coverage. These are, without being too scathing — the

Mulder and Scully brigade that lurk on the edges — the curiosity fringe who are always attracted to the unexplained.

Many people have sought definitive details about the mystery that has drawn so many to Southwold's four shores. The details that exist are sketchy and contradictory. A few extra details have unfolded over the years but these have only served to intensify interest and debate.

If at dusk or early morning, you see someone, especially one with a camera, walking slowly past such a house, they may be one of the few that do know the secret location. They may be someone who may know something about what happened or they may have found someone who really does have a clue.

No one appears to know exactly who was involved or even more intriguingly when it actually occurred but we all know that until the mystery is solved and we find out what actually happened, all of us who are interested in the Southwold Mystery will find it endlessly fascinating to return and look for clues and signs year after year. The Southwold Mystery Shop has some fascinating souvenirs. Sherlock Holmes deerstalker hats are a particular favourite with Japanese visitors.

It is said that some people have actually gone mad and have occasionally been found wandering Southwold streets in the hours before dawn or standing in the waves lost in thought — literally lost at sea never to return to the shores of reality. It is probably true. Anyone of us could get caught up in the sense of excitement such a strange mystery evokes.

A conversation overheard in the Sailors' Reading Room caused a flurry of excitement last year but nothing came of it in the end.

There was a whole section in the museum dedicated to the chronology of events and a collection of artefacts that had been related to the mystery, found over the years. But the timings and findings were in such dispute, by the Mystery Hunters and some very angry residents, that the whole thing was taken down a short time later. There were even a cohort of people who had booked into local hotels in order to see the exhibition who were extremely unhappy to find it had been taken down.

With such informative books as *The Omni House* and *Branes Old Tales* (currently a best seller) not to mention the extraordinary scholarship of *Marne's Table of Amendments* to help us, it is certain that before to long fresh progress will be made and even perhaps a complete breakthrough will soon occur! Let's hope so because there are a growing number of people who desperately want to know and need to discover the truth behind The Southwold Mystery!

The Artefact

People would be queueing around the block if it was generally known what was actually in Southwold's small museum.

The artefact in question is stated to be only a few hundred years old and of unknown origin. Indeed it is not even under lock and key. In some ways it is safer that way — hidden in plain sight as though it is an unremarkable piece of Southwold heritage.

It was one of the earliest museum acquisitions. The whole collection has grown up around it over the years. The artefact's provenance has never been questioned by those in the know. It is well known that there are some original letters. The oldest being from the early 18th century.

The object itself, though relatively unremarkable, is steeped in the mystery fuelled by the disappearance of several families connected to its history. Their names are known by certain Southwold residents still living in the gradually emptying town.

Though the shops are thronged with people, walk slowly along any Southwold back street, stare through a plethora of shadowed vacant interiors and the sheer emptiness of the houses in this thriving town can become disquieting. As someone once said 'it's a bit like a film set of empty front room facades'. Actual full-time residents are few and far between.

Stride along the promenades past brightly coloured huts day after day and it will be hard not to become aware of the lack of family activity — a lack of general usage. The bright paint and jaunty names do not disguise the general feeling that their owners are far away and are not part of the Southwold (shall one say lack of) crowd. It is sometimes hard not to speculate about Southwold houses' empty air. Yet strangely enough for such a small population there is still a thriving school.

So what is known of the aforementioned artefact? I know you are dying to know. And what is known about the disappearance of the families in question? Speculation has centred around one hut in particular — a hut that is unlike the other huts. You will know it when you see it, and say to yourself 'aha that's the one — I knew I would spot it !'

We all give it a surreptitious glance as we pass it. Sometimes strange people no-one has ever seen before have been seen using it in a seemingly normal way, but they do not quite achieve normality. They just look odd and out of place as if they are trying too hard at normality.

It is quite the same when you come across the artefact in the museum. You know it is the artefact because it just does not fit with the rest of the collection in the museum. An air of mystery is quite apparent to even the most down to earth of people. Yet no-one exclaims loudly 'that's it!' They keep it to themselves or whisper speculatively to those they are with. It has been the same ever since the museum opened.

Many people who become intrigued by both the artefact and the hut decide to make the trip to the British Library to read the collection of family letters for themselves. But they remain none the wiser expect for a few unusual details. What happened to the families connected with this strange story remains largely unknown up to the present day.

The hut can be seen in the background of a faded old picture in the Sailors's Reading Room. It is thought to be a relic from the days when the beach was adorned with nets and herring barrels, long before the bathers came. How it has stayed intact since that early picture was taken is one of the things that has fuelled the mystery down the years.

There are rumours that another piece of the artefact was recently found in a boarded attic, charred but still intact. A piece that is, I am reliably informed, undoubtably connected with the artefact because its alignment has been expertly verified, but there has been nothing in the local press about a new donation to the museum.

There has, however, been another interesting development that is thought to be connected to the artefact. I for one did not see the UFO reported by many to have been seen hovering low over the Southwold huts last January. The last mention of anything of a similar nature was in the Southwold letters archive in 1933 that is held in the Suffolk Records Office in Ipswich. This is now thought now to be related to some experimental flying craft. There are several references to strange unexplained occurrences in family letters from the Victorian era. The reference to Gabriella Rossetti's visit to the town one winter is most colourful.

The most interesting reference to such phenomena was in a letter that can be found in the British Library archives dated 1765 along with a woodcut depicting the strange event. That picture, or a replica at least, should really be on display in the Southwold Museum as part of the collection.

However it is probably thought to be too fanciful a part of Southwold's intriguing history and has no doubt been rejected by the museum committee. There have been some rumours down the years that they do not want to display too much. On any given day in Southwold rather odd looking people can be spotted if you look for them. Perhaps they are keeping an eye on things.

The Forgetful Chef

'You have the memory of a sieve on holiday' called his sister May as she rolled her eyes.

He always called her May Bug.

'Just for a lark' he would fib. The truth was that, that was how he remembered she was called May. She was an annoyance, an irreverent giggler who seemed to know everything. God had made a big mistake when He had made her the eldest.

He, himself, should have been the first born and it was beneath his use of brain power to actually remember her name and the 'bug' bit was a delightful little insult. An affectionate brotherly put down each time he used it. A phrase that was window dressing for his inner spite. A spite he relished and enjoyed!

It was just as well he still lived in the small town of Southwold. There was only one winding main street that divided around the small square and met itself again in a loop. When he forgot any part of his extensive cooking ingredients he would stride out purposefully to obtain the missing item, which was often forgotten again by the time he reached the shops. He sometimes tried to write a list but that always got mislaid somehow. As he was a local minor celebrity, people would often stop him in the street and greet him like an old friend.

'Hello TC! They would call out in a friendly manner. Of course it should have been TFC but he forgot the 'Forgetful' F part when he first ordered his signature mugs for the TV show.

After an early live show with a very famous celebrity whose name he couldn't remember, TC decided to get named mugs for every guest. He made a point of having a mug of tea at the start of each show while he discussed the menu with his guest and TV audience. His guests would each have their name written large on their mug so there could be no obvious lapse of memory. He frequently forgot who they were but would take a slurp of tea and refresh his memory by looking at his guest's mug. The mugs were distinctive and came from *Gallery Thea*, the wonderful Southwold pottery, and every guest was given their mug at the end of the show. If there was no guest a member of the invited audience of fans would be delighted to receive a TC mug with his signature joke about forgetting the 'F'.

He could never remember who anyone in Southwold was but he knew he was supposed to know them. That smiling 'Hello' always sent him into an internal panic. Outwardly he would appear cool and slightly detached but inwardly he would feel stress mounting. Again and again they would repeat his name as they continued to chat. This friendly habit would pile on the pressure of his stress at not being able to recall their name and reciprocate by saying their's at appropriate junctures.

In some ways he could have quite easily become a recluse after all the excitement of MI5. But constant trips to the shops kept his urban cosmopolitan side busy. Later he would relax in the sea and sunlight, enjoying walks along Southwold's four shores as he thought up new taste combinations.

As a boy he had played memory games with his sister as they ran along the sand shouting out the names of the huts then go back along blindfold. One guiding — the other struggling to remember the correct sequence of names as they went back. He had a secret book in which he kept list of hut sequences and would secretly memorised them long into the night. His sister almost always won the game even so. She was good at thinking up energetic forfeits for loosing. He could only ever think of one. In winter it was cruel but in late summer she would delight in hitching up her skirt and running into the waves at his command of forfeit. If he counted up to fifty she would come out with blue legs at Christmas. He suspected that she lost deliberately sometimes but only in summer.

The Black Shore was always a favourite haunt. They would play touch tag with friends in the dunes then buy bottles of *Vimto* to swig round the back of the fishing huts. He had forgotten their names but could see them clearly in his mind's eye. None of them had stayed, not even his sister. No, she was long gone and good riddance. He was still angry, still felt betrayed after all these years. She stopped playing so abruptly it had taken him by surprise. Then she had started wearing embarrassing bras and mini skirts and hanging round with people he didn't know. If he went up to her when she was with them she turned away as if she didn't know him. Once he asked her about it but she just rolled her eyes in a grown up way and made a funny sound.

That's when he first took to spying. He would make coded references in notebooks and take surreptitious polaroids of them in the dunes and round the back of pubs. As he got better at it there were snapshots of others, visitors mostly kissing in the dunes. He saved up and bought a pair of sneakers to help his silent approach. Sometimes they were so engrossed in kissing and fondling he could get really close up without them knowing. So he was well suited to his time in MI5. They called him 008 in the service and he was licensed to kill. Forgetting came easy.

The cooking show came later but he could never remember what happened to his sister. He remembered a late night fire on the beach and a feeling of boiling anger with her. Bashing the embers of the fire to smithereens as the dawn came up — kicking sand over the charcoal again and again, he felt dark and alone. He never saw her again after that.

'She's gone off with some lad,' father would say softly, staring into his nightly tipple. But somehow the whole family knew that it wasn't true but no one knew why.

He sometimes tried to remember what had made him so angry that night but he never could recall it. Only bashing the embers of the fire as if his life depended on it had made any sense to him.

His *The Forgetful Chef* cookery programmes had taken him all round the world to obscure places. He would always be cooking outdoors and always forget something and have to make do with what he had, rush to a local shop or find a wild herb to complete the dish. The most watched Christmas Special was when he forgot to put on his trousers. *The Forgetful Chef* became a household name after that.

Part of his memorability with the public was that he would never reveal his name. Certainly the history of his early family life in Southwold seems to have been completely expunged from the records. No one knew where he actually lived. The post office is his postal address. The Lord Nelson

61

or the Swan are his preferred meeting venues. He has no other needs as with mobile and laptop he can live anywhere.

The skills he honed at MI5 have enabled him to avoid any discernible footprint of his casual use of the plethora of empty houses in Southwold. He would take his pick without anyone being the wiser. His own house, an anonymous empty shell with an unkempt garden, was full of his family's old dusty furniture. He would wait until the street was empty before slipping in or out through the side gate. But mostly he delighted in living in the many large empty houses in Southwold free and gratis. Variety is the spice of life after all, he would tell himself. And the slight danger of discovery was mildly exciting. Truth was he needed the adrenaline rush after living in the shadowy world of espionage. It also satisfied his inner chameleon.

Having lived so many false identities it amused him to not have his name on the TV credits. He had spent so much of his life avoiding recognition that he liked to remain anonymous. Being TC was quite enough public exposure.

If anyone came up to him and asked him his real name directly — 'Oh, you can tell me,' they would say.

'I forgot it years ago!' He would respond.

This may or may not have been true. As the years advanced he could be seen, if one rose at dawn, slowly walking along looking at the names of the Southwold huts or staring out to sea from the dunes as if trying to remember... or trying to forget.

Peregrine Fellows

Peregrine Fellowes always had on the same — 'I wore it when I met Ted Hughes' hat.

'Got it in Southwold. I bought it in Denny's yonks ago, back in the dim and distant,' he would say with his slightly secretive, old boys in the know, smile.

For years he had sat in the same 'I always get there ahead of the rush', chair, under the corner light at the Isambard Kingdom Public House at the unfashionable end of King's Road.

Young people entered the Kingdom Pub with a sense of wonder that it hadn't been pine-table-eatery-changed since the swinging Sixties.

'It was unbelievably swinging!' Peregrine would answer with a twinkle in his eye if anyone asked. 'I happen to have a Sixties poem with me — would you like to hear it? Mine's a pint.'

He would take off a thick elastic band and rifle through his large note books. 'A bit dog eared like me,' he would smile.

Peregrine was the reason the pub had survived. 'His people had money, the lucky tosser,' was the goss.

'My people are all gone. We lived by the sea at Southwold. I am the last of the line,' he would say with mock moroseness as he toasted the Muse. Privately his set thought he was lucky to get Aubrey to publish *Slim Volume.* Conversely his readings were well attended by the Chelsea Arts Club crowd.

His flat around the corner, 'I've been there since the Ark,' came with the pub. Only Peregrine knew it was there.

Everyone else had forgotten where the door in the wall led to. Even Scroggins grandson, who now ran the pub, had forgotten the flat.

'We humour the old codger.'

The cost-an-arm-an-a-leg lawyers had told Scroggins he couldn't change a thing in the Isambard Kingdom. 'Without that damn old lush's consent'.

Anyway Scroggins was shrug-shoulders lazy. 'As long as the punters come in I don't mind.'

Peregrine's faded pub chair was surrounded by some elegant '50s framed photos. 'Old and dear friends actually. We partied all night and then had breakfast at Picasso's.'

'That's an interesting picture!'

Peregrine was jerked out of his, I-can-see-them-all-clear-as-day, reverie.

A young man pointed to a black and white snap of Peregrine complete with his old hat in the club with Marilyn.

'Her smile could light up the room. We were with Arthur Miller that night.'

The AC/DC Boy was pictured posing with one arm around Peregrine, his other arm casually draped around Marilyn.

Having the photo up there with The Boy in public view was, he knew, rather risky. But he so loved the memory of that night, dancing wildly with Marilyn and The Boy.

He gave the young man an overly bright — I thought I'd got away with it — it was years ago' smile.

'Yes dear boy, Marilyn's smile is hard to miss. I sewed her into that dress that night you know.'

Peregrine thought about how he had sewn up the sack and noticed his hands were shaking a little.

'So you're quite handy with a needle and thread? May I?'

The young man pulled up an adjacent chair.

'Of course, dear boy' enthusiasm in the charm of his voice but not in his heart. This modern young man looked so similar to The Boy.

He looked like a young Greek god.

'He was my uncle'

'Who?'

'Uncle Jack — in the photo with Marilyn.'

'I never knew his real name. We all called him *The Boy*.'

'We did some digging recently'

Peregrine looked alarmed.

'Digging? Where?'

Steady — steady. Keep calm don't give anything away.

'Family Archives. We're trying to find out what happened to him.'

'I haven't a clue! Not a clue! He just disappeared. I was heartbroken.'

'So you've no idea where he went?'

Peregrine took a swig of his beer. Not to Heaven certainly.

'It was so long ago. More years than I care to remember.'

Who could forget his sleek young torso. Alan Turing had turned up that night. We were all great friends. The Boy took quite a shine to Alan I remember. Quite a shine — had rather a row about it actually.

'I never saw him again,' he said out loud.

He said such vile and hurtful things — Peregrine's hands clenched in a spasm of anger and hurt.

Peregrine fingered the silver top of his ebony stick — I was incandescent. There was so much blood!

'Gran will be pleased I tracked you down.'

'I never knew he had family — never spoke about his past, only his future…'

'We'd like a copy of that photo if you didn't mind — for our family archives.'

'Yes. Yes. Come again. I'll have one ready for you. Come in next week — do.'

Peregrine smiled as uncharacteristically early he got up to go.

Back at his high-ceilinged flat he lit the fire. — God it can be cold in June!

He went to the bureau and brought out a drawer full of their photos.

The one with The Boy naked wearing his old pheasant feather hat at a rakish angle, produced a tear of self pity that rolled down Peregrine's cheek.

The lines of their naked young bodies entwined together were so very beautiful — but what if there were questions?

Crimes that happened long ago were coming to light these days. Was there still DNA held deep in the indented patterned grooves of his silver topped cane?

Slowly Peregrine Fellows ignited his colourful past to the flames of his funeral pyre.

He never left his flat again.

Mother

Peregrine Fellows Part 2

Mother was an absolute gem! As a boy I worshipped the ground she walked on.

She was marvellously eccentric. Everyone said so. I could never see it. Mother was just Mother to me.

Her Southwold dinner parties were legendary.

'Scrummy left-overs Mother!'

'Cook always excels herself,' Mother would say in her rather dismissive way. Mother had done Cordon Bleu in her debutant days.

I always knew by the way she said it, she could do a better job than cook if she had the time.

Mother simply loved her arrangements. Everything had its perfect spot. If anything got rearranged things would suddenly go dark. I quite thought Mother had God-like powers when I was very small. Lights would go out and curtains snap shut if I displeased her in any way. I still don't like the dark.

I remember as a tiny tot climbing up on a chair and pulling a cord switch — dark/light, dark/light, off/on, off/on. Just like one of Mother's brilliant red lipstick smiles and her snap-shut gold compact with its soft smelling powder puff. Click open — shut click—open click—shut. That was Mother to a T!

But she had this phrase 'I'll put you in the trunk and send you to Perou!' Then I knew I was for it.

I can still see that trunk. It made me widdle when I was small, just when I passed it on the landing.

I don't think I ever got to Perou. But she put me in there for a long time! It seemed forever sometimes in the dark.

Nanny rescued me occasionally, even though Mother told her not to. I think I whimpered a bit. I still don't like hearing dogs making that sound. It was character-building of course. Talk of Brazil still gives me the shivers. Funny that, after all this time.

Mother looked rather like that Wallace Simpson woman. Never a hair out of place — Dior dresses and riding in jodhpurs. Tremendously stylish she was. I used to try on her shoes, her lipstick and rouge, dressing up.

When they came back from abroad, if anything was out of place, she would know - and she'd know who. I found one of her wigs left out in her room on a wig stand one time. Tilly , her maid, must have left it out. Up until then I thought her hair was real. It gave me quite a turn to see it on the wig stand. It was as if it was Mother but with an empty face.

I rarely saw Father. Never really knew him of course. One didn't in those days — just wasn't done. Only Sunday luncheon after church if he was back. He would hold forth about his golf or a shoot or some motoring escapade in his silver blue Bugatti — marvellous stuff.

He would give me a bloody good hiding if I'd upset Mother — left a toy on the stairs or something — or when I took off. I got in the habit of it, rather. It frightened Mother, of course, if I went for days. Sometimes I couldn't help myself. I just had to breathe in the wind and the high Suffolk skies. I would run to the place I called Edge of the World, which was to an old house miles inland. It had dark rhododendron lakes inhabited by, *The Fish Gods,* as I called them.

For the most part I explored closer to home. Dark at night, Reydon woods were. Foxes screaming would make me jump but I felt quite safe mostly in my secret stick wigwam playing Hiawatha. I love that poem of Longfellow's. Do you know it?

Wonderful stuff! Haven't thought of it in years. I knew most of it by heart. It was *Hiawatha* that started me on poetry. I'd run through the woods Indian style, my penknife in my pocket with my whittled bow and arrow, running with the tom-tom drumbeat of the lines, barefoot, sometimes with a pheasant feather in my hair.

By the shores of Gitche Gumee

By the shining Big-Sea-Water,

Stood the wigwam of Nokomis,

Daughter of the Moon, Nokomis.

At the door on summer evenings

Sat the little Hiawatha

Heard the whispering of the pine-trees

Heard the lapping of the waters,

Sounds of music, words of wonder

'Minne-wawa!' said the Pine-trees

'Mudway-aushka!' said the water.

Marvellous fun!

Then of course there was that trouble with the charcoal burners and I was sent off to board at St Felix in Southwold. My parents went travelling abroad .

I missed Mother but I'd grown out of Nannie.

Nine was a very good age to start boarding Mother said.

The Charcoal Burners

Peregrine Fellows Part 3

'What a caper that was! The charcoal burners! Some of it is a bit hazy. Long time ago you see.

They live in turf huts. Did you know that? Mud huts that look like upturned bowls. They made them from turf. Made the same way they made the charcoal burning mound in the middle of every temporary settlements.

I smelt the smoke. That's what drew me away so far from home the first time. It came on the breeze.

I followed it through the coppice woods — I had never been so far but I wanted to find the source — the fire source. I couldn't make out where it was at first because there was no wind. The smoke drifted slowly, mysteriously through the trees. Then I found them.

Faces blackened, deep lined and bright jewel eyes, black cuffs and trousers frayed. Quiet spoken they were, though mostly silent in their work of stacked wood. The mound had to be sealed for a slow burn.

'The secret is no air. Once embers are in we close it up an' wait.'

Joe was his name, the one who spoke to me. A gentle voice he had and manner too.

Thin as a whippet he was. He shook my hand. I can still feel the roughness of that hand. He looked me in the eye as if I was a man already. I felt proud to be his friend and sit to watch the smoke with him. It was sheer delight to see him using his billhook to coppice tree limbs or take out his knife from his large leather belt to carve a clothes peg. I shall never forget that smell of smokey clothes and fresh cut wood.

'Us charcoal burners stay on till the job's done,' he said. 'Then we move on to another patch of wood or another wood entirely.'

They moved on but were back the next year. Something happened the second time they came.

I had made a map that winter, a map so I could find them again.

I put it in my poem *Wood Smoke and Ashes*. Do you know it? It won the Ted Hughes Prize one year.

I went on a recce the next spring, just to see, just to make sure I could find them again. I got to the clearing and poked about a bit, saw some birds and found some charcoal sticks for drawing.

A blackened kingdom in the woods. It was magic — haunting — empty. I looked through doorways and found a tiffin can. I got to know those woods quite well. Then one afternoon I smelt smoke again. I fairly ran along the path and Joe swung me up onto a branch to watch them at their work.

Well, Mother must have seen Joe walk me home along— arm in arm we were. I'd spent a night away. I didn't think she'd really notice.

Such an adventure it was to sleep in the clearing near Joe's hut. He'd slept under the moon that night — showed me Orion in the stars. He said our futures were written in the stars and he knew the writing.

74

We'd seen an owl, all ghostly, glide low across the camp as we ate our fried spam. A fox kept crying deep into the night.

'Like a lost soul' Joe said.

I didn't let on I lived in the big house. Even though we went through the kitchen garden and I pulled some onions for Joe to take back to camp. I suppose my face was quite smoke smudged and I'd torn my shirt a bit. Well, Mother was livid.

She shouted at Joe with her bright red mouth. I tried to explain and so did Joe but she said she'd get Mr Hebditch, our town Bobby, to see him off. I don't know if she did but I was put on bread and water and sent to my room for days.

Father came back from his office in London and gave me a hiding for staying in the clearing with the men. Mother had got him on the blower straight away.

'Whitehall 357' I'll never forget the slowly whirring dial sounds as she rang that number. Her voice was so cold it chilled my spine.

I told Father I wanted to be a charcoal burner when I grew up but that just made things worse I think.

They got our horrid vicar — Father Lee, to tutor me before they sent me off to board that autumn. He got me in the book cupboard. His hot breath smelt of rum and smokes. He mumbled that he'd been a sailor once.

I never saw the charcoal burners again. I looked for them in the clearing whenever I got back but never saw them. I left a note in a bottle in Joe's hut one time but I doubt if he could read, except for reading stars.

Lucan in Southwold

Peregrine Fellows Part 4

Well, yes, Lucky Lucan was a bit of a mate of mine around the Soho clubs.

Ronnie Scott's was a particular haunt of ours in the whisky smoke of the wee small hours.

I knew something was up when he called me from a pay phone in the middle of the night, said he was in a bit of a tight spot. His name was in the papers for days.

He told us he was innocent and because he was our friend we quite believed him to be a man of his word. Although it did look bad in the papers. But you can't cross question an old chum — can you? So we helped obscure his trail.

I got an enigmatic card from Bogota one time, but after the boat incident I wasn't interested, wasn't interested at all! After all he'd left me for dead in the boat we borrowed from our old chum Mackenzie.

My family still have the house on Gun Hill. Empty most of the year, of course. That's where Lucan hid out for a bit while we arranged things. No one would think to look for him in Southwold.

Well, after we set sail. We began celebrating his escape. Typical of Lucky Lucan that was! He'd smuggled a magnum of champagne aboard. The conversation got rather heated in the middle of our voyage. We were in the cabin having a refill of champers.

I had seen something in the papers I wanted to ask him about. I quite forget now what it was. I had never seen him really angry. I remember the change in his eyes — wolf eyes! I changed the subject.

By the time we were in sight of the Dutch coast we were both in our cups. He must have hit me on the head and swum for the shore. He always was a damn fine swimmer.

By the time I came to, feeling groggy, the boat was taking in water. I had to bail like hell. I almost didn't make it back. He could have left me the bloody charts!

We all knew Lucky Lucan was a ladies' man and a gambler. We knew he had a temper but never would have thought it of him to leave me for dead like that. I finally managed to sail into Southwold's Black Shore. Appropriate really. Lucky Lucan was a scoundrel and no mistake!

There is no evidence that Lucky Lord Lucan hid in Southwold but there are various houses that could, perhaps, have been perfect hideouts.

Princess Sophia Dhuleep Singh selling "The Suffragette" outside Hampton Court Palace, where she has a suite of apartments.

Princess Raj

We live in Southwold, which is one of the most easterly towns in England. Many of us have collected here like the flotsam and jetsam of an exotic wreck from the British Raj — left here on this eastern-most English shore.

It is whimsical, I know, but I but I believe we need to be as close as possible, geographically speaking, to India's pearlescent light. We are undoubtedly all rather prone to staring towards the east across the ruffled waves. Yearning, perhaps, for the Indian sub continent we were drawn to by luck or favour. We are all *posh — port out and starboard home*, as we say — to ensure the best cabins on those arduous sea journeys to and from India.

Many of us can be found on the Southwold promenades watching the waves. I believe it is because we have all spent time contemplating the vastness of the ocean on our long sea voyages back and forth. Only now we voyage on HMS Southwold and can play croquet on her lawns. All of us seek out the plentiful Suffolk sun, though it is weak compared to the blaze of India.

In our little Raj enclave we understand Queen Victoria, our Empress of India, has engaged the special service that Abdul Karim provides for her in her older age. May God preserve her in her colourful choice of escort. To most of our British Islanders it is a scandal. But many of us have brought our Indian servants to be with us. Their colour and their gentle pride sustains us. We simply must have kedgeree, our own Raj curries and Indian tea. We deem it a fine thing to have a small East India Company crammer in the town.

We always love to see her, Sophia Singh, the Queen's dearest Goddaughter strolling along with her little entourage. Quite a sight she is in the latest London fashions. We always feel especially blest when she is amongst us and some of us have more than a nodding acquaintance with her.

She usually arrives by train — so very much the latest way to travel. And so for several weeks we enjoy her presence in our midst. Of course we all secretly hope the Queen might join her. Sophia is quite the Royal favourite. But our Queen is getting on in years and the journey is quite long from London, even by train.

Among ourselves we affectionately call her Princess Raj, because, of course, we now know she is Sophia Duleep Singh, daughter of a Maharaja. Her brother has an estate near Thetford and sometimes brings her in his motor vehicle.

Of course the first time she arrived she was quite the mystery woman as we did not know of her illustrious connections. But Lady Winstanley saw her at a gathering at the palace and Mrs Abercrombie showed some of us her pictured in the London Gazette. It was around the time Abdul Karim had actually danced with the Queen and caused rather a stir.

Some say Sophia's sister has studied to become a doctor in America but we can hardly credit this as possible. How could any woman ever hope to gain such a vast body of knowledge — let alone actually prescribe medicines?

It is also rumoured Sophia is a suffragette which is altogether too modern for many of us Southwold ladies.

Ghost Ship

Generations of my family have lived on these shores 'tis said since doomsday, but I dunno the truth of that.

I have seen ghosts in our house — all of 'em friendly. I've felt the shivers of course. We all go cold when we see them. Ghosts do that to a body.

It's a strange thing, even to me, but ever since I were a lad I've been looking for something. It's as if a secret had been whispered in my ear by one of them, as if I'd been told to find something but they hadn't told me what I was looking for.

It seemed to the family that one of them had lost something 'cos we'd often return to find the house disrupted — drawers turned out and the like. I dunno why people are afeared so much of ghosts, 'tis normal for us to see them now and again especially in the cold dark winter months but the long summer nights can draw them out as well as I will now unfold.

The time I like the best in the year is August. The girls wear their lightest muslin dresses in August. They look so fetching walking along in the sunshine.

At night the moon is as big as a plate, so bright as to be dazzling. The night waves role in with lights inside, phosphorus 'tis called. To me 'tis a magic thing to see, as the water lights-up around our legs and oars. 'Tis movement that makes the light appear.

On big moon nights I cannot sleep for seeing so much brightness in the night.

Now people ask me was I or was I not afeared that time, the time that I do tell of, round the bar. The time I saw more than you could shake a stick at, in terms of ghosts. Truth is I was in fear at first and then so much was happening I forgot my fears and got curious and amazed. But as you will hear the fear did come again. Such fear as has changed the course of my life.

I have never been out on the high seas since. I sold me skiff and made our parlour into a bar. Same as the Ale Wives on the London Road in Wangford. 'Twas Flossy Tanner in Wangford who taught me how to brew ale. She always had an eye for me, did Floss.

People come to Southwold now for to take the sea air for their ailments and the like. Our little village needed a public house and there were just enough customers in the winter months to warrant it. Quite a few are settling from foreign parts. Our little village is growing fast. There is even talk of a railway station!

So my brother and I went into the brewery trade and made our first ale that were supped with satisfaction by many. But it were that August night that changed everything.

Well, I was fishing in me skiff up near Benacre when I heard laughter. 'Tis true. Laughter came first, clear across the water that were still as a millpond that night.

Next me skiff were near turned over. As a great olden time ship reared up out of the water covered in the strangeness of the phosphorescent light. Me boat was bucking up and down the swell but I was still. Iron still, wishing I could move my hands and arms to row away. But I were frozen to ice it seemed. The top mast reached up as high as the moon it seemed to me. A moon the size of a dinner plate it was that night.

In a few minutes the laughter turned to snarls and shouts.

There was the sound of clashing metal and someone must have got punched 'cos a large front tooth dropped over the side of the ship into me skiff. There it was, white with moonlight, black with blood.

Still I couldn't move. Coins flew over the great bow of the ship like so much rain and some of it landed in the skiff. A n ugly head looked over the bow with a shout of rage. The hairs on the back of my neck stood up as I thought I was seen. A flagon of ale bobbed past me, between me and the tall ship. I grabbed it an' took a swig. Second nature that was!

Best ale I ever tasted and swigging it got me moving. I grabbed the oars and rowed away, coins were glinting in the bottom of the skiff.

When I looked up of a sudden it had gone. That whole great ship had disappeared! Nothing was there. The sea was empty except for moonlit waves. Even so I got my skiff back in harbour double quick. That flagon of ale steadied me nerves all the way back.

I keep it here above the bar. 'Tis my evidence of that strange night. Though some do say 'tis never true, but I do say 'have you ever seen such a flagon as this in these here parts? Find me one like it an' you can call me a liar!'

No one ever has seen it's like for sure. An' I sup me beer from it to this day.

The ancient coins I sold to an old army major who lived here for a while. He took them to London. So I got a good price when all's said and done. Bought the oak bar with that money we did.

I kept just one coin for remembrance and the tooth that dropped into my skiff that night in a special bag for years and then somehow it was not there. The bag was empty an' I searched high and low to this day but cannot find the coin or the tooth now. Funny thing though, our house ghosts have stopped their mayhem. M'ebbe they found what they was looking for in all those years before!

All I know is I likes my ale an' I keep trying to create a brew as good as the one I tasted from this here flagon, on that strange night. Somehow though I can never brew an ale that's quite as good as I remember. But this one called 'Ghost Ship' is very like it. Very like.

Queen Victoria's Bucket

There are several speculations as to why Salty Fisher's picture no longer hangs in the Sailors' Reading Room. His exploits were many and various and at one time he was the toast of the town due to his daring rescue of Molly Hobart from the fire that ravaged Church Close, back in the day. Indeed there was a parade held in his honour for many a year after that.

It was said that Salty got together the team of *Bucketeers* that stopped the fire from taking hold of St. Edmund's Church (that and the Reverend Hobart's praying).

The *Bucket Parade* became the highlight of the Southwold year, back in the day. Every one of the Bucketeers, men and quite a few women, were given a small silver coloured bucket presented in honour of the line they had held. Even Queen Victoria knew about it up in her palace in London.

It was down to Princess Raj that the Queen's Bucket got presented to Southwold. She were the Queen's favourite goddaughter and she visited Southwold on account of her old nanny living in Church Street. They did manage to save all of the old ones and some of the worker families that were carving the angels. But what ever happened to Queen Victoria's Bucket is another Southwold mystery.

'Tis said that the actual presentation got a few grins when Queen Victoria's Bucket was presented to the mayor from the Queen herself and inscribed to Salty and all of us 'Towns People of Southwold' for our bravery. Every man jack of us had buckets in those days 'cos there were no such thing as plumbing. Well, there was a newfangled thing called a

Thunder Box for the Reverend and some as had gold in their pockets. But the 'Bucketeers', as we were ever after called, were humble fisher folk, most of us had used our own night soil buckets in the line. Hours it took to save the church and it was a near run thing.

Old Salty Fisher was a natural born leader and he kept the line intact more or less. 'Tis said when Squinty Saunders and his son with the bad leg dropped out, their old woman took over. She were stronger than they, 'tho she were seventy year or more.

So the idea of the Salty's Silver Bucket parade took hold. Every child was handed a little tin bucket of flowers to give to the ladies and a free barrel of beer was pitched on the green by St Ed's for the men. This was on account of the brewery being saved as well as the church and o'course the beer was used in dousing the fire as well, but some was used to keep spirits up. It is probably true that the men were conflicted between which one to save at first — the church or the brewery. But Salty Fisher was the toast of Southwold because he saved both. He got a line to the beach and buckets were filled with sand, they say, and some with water. The young'ns ran along with lanterns as the buckets were passed from hand to hand.

Quite a sight that night it must have been. The whole town turned out to make our Southwold safe. And the children still run from the beach to the town with torches as it gets dark in remembrance of that terrible night. 'Twas a miracle they got that Princess Raj's nanny out. Salty got a ladder that went up in flames just after he had carried her down.

The old sailors still gather in the Sailors' on Tuesdays remembering their past days. They speculate as to which one of his sweethearts took Old Salty's picture. T'was taken in one of those newfangled photographic picture boxes. Squinty Saunders swears it was the artist's daughter from London, the one that came up with William Morris' lot. Several summers they stayed and there were some right goings on. 'Tis said Mr Morris cried on the beach for a week when his wife ran off with that Rossetti fellow. That were the subject of a fair old mardle it has to be said. But there is something in what Squinty says, because it's a cause for pride that that Princess Raj asked to borrow the picture to show his likeness to our Queen Victoria herself God bless her. Maybe Salty's picture never got returned to its rightful place on the Sailor's Reading Room wall after that, no one ever could remember.

Of course there are other stories 'bout Salty and our vicar's daughter, as well as him starting the ferry service for the visitors on account of him wanting to visit the Walberswick Widow. She lived in the black hut by the shore and was very tall for a women. They say she were an artist too, an' Salty, with his strong arms would row her up the Blyth on moonlit nights. But that's the women talking. The old boys wink and chuckle into their beer and tell a far more bawdy tale — one of burning flares upriver and naked bodies on dark nights. The truth may lie somewhere between but 'tis the telling of the old tales that causes their eyes to brighten.

As to the mystery of why his picture no longer hangs in the reading room. It still is a matter of speculation for those that knew him as to which one of his sweethearts took it.

He were lost in a storm up near Iceland. T'is true they went that far, back in the day.

One things for certain Salty Fisher's exploits will never be forgotten or 'never in this world' as they say.

It is well known that visiting Walberswick was fashionable for many artists in the Victorian era and there are many pictures of sailors in Southwold Sailors' Reading Room.

Southwold Sailors
The Reading Room Opening Day 1864

Tossed in storms they were and biting east wind cold. Screaming sometimes as it tore into hair, loose oil skin and sail. Gales buffeted their heaving bucking boats. Strong faces turned towards salty tearing blasts of Arctic air. The chilling dangers of the vast dark churning waves

Better at reading clouds and stars, they had applied themselves to letters. Some more than others if truth be told. But Mrs Rayley had given them a place of quietude and temperance.

Intoned on opening day - in terms they understood

> "A long pull
>
> And a strong pull
>
> And a pull together
>
> Securing benefit and hearts rejoicing,"

is what the reverend said.

"And so we shall lads — so we shall. A place to meet and read the occurrences of the day. Storms may rage outside. Inside is quiet, peace and safety."

A place for sailors' yarns and visitors alike. A room set adrift a century and a half ago, complete with replicated boats. Held encased in moments, on the tide of time.

Fragments of men's lives are saved for us to savour how they lived. To gather fish and hoist the sails and head for home and shelter.

William Morris in Southwold

The Treasure Hunt & Christina Rossetti's Southwold Christmas

The Treasure Hunt

Very few people know that William Morris took a house for several seasons in Southwold — 1867 and 1868 to be precise. Even fewer witnessed his tears from a broken heart dropped into the Southwold sand dunes. He felt a kindred spirit with Arthur Pendragon. His Guinevere had lost her heart to Rossetti that summer.

He had become painfully aware of their long disappearance during the Southwold treasure hunt afternoon, as the shadows lengthened into evening. The first treasure hunt had been Rossetti's idea. It had taken place in Bloomsbury. Another at the Red House had been organised by Morris himself and the treasures were usually encased in Morris' patterned fabric bags. The treasure hunt at Southwold was a charity event.

Had Rossetti suggested it? Morris wracked his brains as he stared miserably out to sea, occasionally dabbing his tears with his red silk handkerchief.

The day had begun with great excitement. The whole household had dressed in medieval garb, as they often did on special occasions. Christina had drawn a passable self portrait in pencil and wash. It was generally agreed that she was becoming an accomplished artist.

The treasures provided for the afternoon were always provided by Morris himself. Little lace handkerchiefs tied up with ribbon, lavender bags and ribbon, woven lavender rattles to put in winter drawers had been made in the village. Several long Japanese silk scarves were quite the best of prizes as these had come from *The Mikado*. Morris had designed some of the fabrics for Gilbert and Sullivan's exuberant musical extravaganza and he had kept some keepsakes when the show had ended. He had designed large wooden blocks for swathes of Japanese fabrics and wrapped them in brightly coloured papers imported from Japan for the treasure hunters to find.

The Southwold Treasure hunt continued in some form for many years. There have been calls for the day to be revived in modern times, it was, after all, an event that drew the artistic and fashionable crowd from London. It was deemed an honour to be asked to donate an 'artefact' for the hunt. Donated by both local and London artists, many small but valuable pieces of 'found' treasure grace the walls and mantle pieces of Southwold to this day.

William Morris rented a house for several months over two years in Southwold. His designs were used for Gilbert and Sullivan's opera The Mikado. *He also spent 20 years trying to preserve the interior of Blythburgh church — known as the* Cathedral of the Marshes.

Christina Rossetti's Christmas

In that bleak midwinter, frosty wind made moaning sounds around the corners of his seaside house We'd come with William, our dear friend Morris for Christmas.

One sparkling winter's morning I had cause to know the hardness of the frosted earth as I slipped and felt the harshness of stone cold ice. Quite bruised, I had to return to the house William had rented for us all.

We became completely snowed in. Snow kept falling. Snow on snow as I stepped out carefully treading in William's footprints through the ringing snow flecked air towards the angel church that Christmas morning, long ago.

Our little party stood before the crib as if we were visiting kings dressed in our velvet fur trimmed robes. We left our little gifts for the poor of Southwold, some of whom lived in hovels on the beach.

In an eternal moment I was there in the stable with the Christ child. I felt the immensity of the presence of the Christ Child before me. While high in the church rafters the roof angels had gathered and were gazing down as our voices swelled towards them. We smiled at the joy of it — the living joy of Christmas.

Yet there was cold and sadness in William's house despite the fire flames which licked with anger against the darkness of coal. William talked morosely of the summer when Jane left him. His return to experience Southwold winter spoke of the cold that gripped the natural warmth of his heart.

Later he told me he wanted to save the extraordinary patrolling Blythburgh angels. How in his pacing despair up and down the aisle, the angels had seemingly changed direction and each time flowed towards him along the vaulted roof. In that empty church echoing the emptiness that he now felt in life without Jane, the silent angels gave him solace.

He talked of visiting Iceland to gather old Norse tales and to experience a deeper intensity of cold. The stories of nordic Herring Buss ships moored at Southwold had excited his interest.

I was shocked by the turn of events my brother had engendered. Charles Howell was the 'postie' between him and Janey that Southwold summer. Howell the rat that had gnawed at edges of William's life. William who gave his full summer heart to all, was now so bleak in winter.

I began writing a few lines of a poem in candle light as the snow fell in the dark of night. Later it became a hymn.

Ghost Homes

There are, without doubt, too many ghost homes in Southwold but as far as I know there are only two ghosts — and they don't speak to each other. Not that that is remarkable in itself, because ghosts usually wish to talk to the living.

And how can it be that I know they do not communicate to each other, either on this side or the other? It is because I am their go-between!

The blind houses they mainly inhabit have long overgrown gardens that are divided by a crumbling wall. I live in two bramble covered sheds at the bottom of their gardens and make a fair living doing odd jobs around the town.

Their ghostly feud started way back along. I was nipper when our house was hit by a stray bomb. The living said I drifted for days in *the comatose state*. I recovered slowly, even though there was nothing to come back for, as my family was all gone up in the bomb. I reckon I met the pair of those ghosts in that place, which is where the living said I had been in lying in Southwold's hospital for weeks. And somehow I got more attached to them ghosts than to the living.

They would hate it if they knew I thought of them as a pair! They might combust and my life would be that much lonelier and easier at times, 'specially when they're quietly fuming.

Anyway I know they keep the status quo. They keep the blind houses empty and I can keep my sheds and my Southwold life.

It is another country — *the comatose state* — I shall never forget it. But it is strangely put together in my mind — as if the pieces barely fit. Nearest as I can get to it, is that it was like a giant mirror, reflective of this world and the next. These worlds that got shaken up together rather like those pretty kaleidoscope things that children have. One of those got left in the playroom of the upper house. I kept it for years in the sheds till it got rusty and fell apart. That strange *Looking Glass* book was there too, in one of the nurseries. A book which I read and reread being the only book I read after the bomb had deafened me. Anyways, that is where I met them — the ghosts.

Neither of them spoke to the other even then. As far as I can tell they blamed each other for what happened. Damn near killed themselves in life and got tangled in their anger strands, like underwater weeds, in death — weeds that can pull a body down. They clearly have forgot the things that made them mad as hell in life. I ask them, and neither of them seem to know what either did to create such hellish rage between them that now persists in shredded ramblings in their after-life. God knows I cannot free them from it. I have tried. But sadly having forgot the causes, they cannot be unravelled. I don't know when or why they died. Maybe it was the same bomb got them as well, mid quarrel.

It's in the paper about ghost houses and the Rich Ones that buy them all up and make the town so full of empty spaces. It makes me worried more ghosts will come. I have enough trouble with two of them.

Southwold is full of rooms that don't fully exist. The living try not to feel it, but the blind rooms keep the emptiness within

them. The living can feel it, even if they try not to do so. It makes them shiver sometimes. I see it when I'm doing their repairs.

I have lots of keys. I keep them in an old seed box. I wander in and out of places doing jobs. I get bought a pint sometimes in The Nelson, by the sea.

The ghosts listen to me in the darkness. I am the only living one that hears them — seems to me. The modern world is deaf.

Emptiness is taking over Southwold. Emptiness in Southwold is worth a million pounds or more. Money grows in emptiness. Maybe emptiness grows in money, too. They say you can smell money but do you know the smell of ghosts?

Many, on entering certain old houses, have smelt that quite distinctive smell that leaks from ghosts, A smell that leaches out from the walls that they pass through. The living are, for the most part, unaware of what the odour portends, but merely find themselves uneasy. It is a smell of otherness and if you think back you will recall it.

It's a growing trend in Southwold. Empty houses.

Southwold Punch

That's the way to do it. Judy, Judy, Judy.

Not mad. Not mad. Not!

Am, am, am! Well, well, well — not well!

Wham! Slam! — That's the way to do it.

And I bow to the audience on this side — then to the other side. Where's the baby? Where's my sticky red stick! Sticky — sticky underfoot.

Are you having fun children?

That's the way to do it. Isn't it children.

Who's behind me? Who? The crocodile? Behind me! Where? Where?

I look here and then over here — no, no, no! Naughty children! There's no one behind me. Oh no there isn't. Is — Isn't. Ow! It bit me. Naughty naughty crocodile! Where's my big sticky stick? Bang, bang, bang. That's the way to do it. Let's get more sausages. Out you go with your bitey teeth!

Eat the sausages. Eat the lot! Oh deary, deary, me.

Judy, Judy, Judy. Mincing, mincing up the Judy. Mrs Punch is sausages!

Mrs Punch is sausages!

Who said that? Was not — Was not — Was not me! Was, was. I didn't , didn't — did ! Oh deary, deary, me — I am in a muddle.

Dee, dah, dee, dah, that's the way to do it!

Mr Plod is knocking on at the door. Run, run. On the run.

*   *   *   *

A small boy's brain is shredded into scattered pieces. Screaming into darkness. Torn from Mum — Mum!

Tearing the homespun fabric years. Torn into tears that overflow the frightened eyes. Open in the darkness.

No Dad No! Into the dark earth potato sack — potatoes emptied into a car boot. Kicking out — trying to escape — trying to reach her, reaching back through the darkness. Mum!

Threatened into silence by stunning blows. A small boy cowers. Curled into the bottom of a sack. Smelling earth. Then urine as trousers flood with warmth. Waking later — ears ringing.

On the road the years are turning. Boy feels angry at Mum. 'For being weak' Dad says. For making Dad angry. For hearing searing condemnation of her easy ways. It's her fault Dad drinks — her fault he's in this stinking sack. He wakes again in shivering silence.

Dad, Dad? No reply.

Occasionally fed. Treated like a dog in need of rescue.

Dad cushions his head in a mockery of love that stifles breath. A bear hug squeeze, a vice-fierce hug, distorting a small boy's rib cage, changing the shape and growth of his heart.

Years later and too late he's dumped on mother's doorstep. He despises his brothers' soft, quiet ways. Brain box – I'll brain your box. I'll throw you rocks. I'll box your ears and take the jeers. I know your fears. I know the fears that make your tears. I'll make your tears for all the years. Be a man now — if you can. You hide, you hide, your hide I'll tan.

Until the silt builds up. Darkly layered. Layer on layer of curdled thought. Of dark thoughts knocked about his concussed, Dad cussed, brain.

Having hurt and hurting he walks away.

Weeks of coastal drifting one day into the next.

One sun filled day he finds the shadow on the sand. A small stripy castle encircled by children watching the dark king of the stripy shack.

Draw the children into your world Professor. Punch, Punch, Punch. Knock 'em dead until they're bled and stain the sand with laughter.

That's the way to do it. Bash the baby. Bash Mrs Punch. She's only a puppet made to be bashed.

Oh! The baby is crying and it must, must, must be bang, bash, stopped.

Aha! All is peace and quiet children. There is always the crocodile with the toothy grim grin. His mouth a black hole space sucker that leaps out and grabs the darkness inside. Land seeps into marshland, sucking it's struggling victims dark dark down.

'Potato head!' They shout at the hunched teen hood. Towards the unseeing dulled down eyes of a schoolyard playground puppet.

Glasses darken. Glasses darken eyes in pain from glaring, cauterising sun, as he's twisted tightly turning into a glaring boy. A son so small. So very small. Looming over the shaking shivering creature that he and they have made.

A growing threatening storm shadow is spinning into the weave. Deeply embedded like a festering thorn.

Whisky yelling breath and gin for quieting. Daren't breathe.

A hungry boy sits watching on the sand. Watching the stripy tent set up. Watching the hiding Punch professor, his voice disguised in harshness, inside his stripy theatre box.

Always hunch-back, always smiling a leering smile. Always innocent of crimes. Punch is the king and fool with a hardened smile. A hardened, leering smile that knows.

They see it all — the little children. Violent grooming stickily absorbed like sherbet on the tongue. Clever, clever, clever.

That's the way to do it. Bash, bash, bash! That's the way to do it.

Oh no I didn't. Did, didn't, did. Confusing little minds.

Hello boys… and girls.

*   *   *   *

102

One day the boy has grown, as has his shadow, into a dark young man. All grown up — but twisted inside into small hard scrumpled pieces. The Sand Professor knows him and takes him into his world of red stripes. Hot panting breath of familiar pain in shadow.

Inside the small striped tent there is familiar hurt. Feeling him over time there is penetration.

'That's the way to do it!'

One night at High Moon, sky drifts slowly over a monstrous shape under the darkening pier of strutted shadows. There is a cooling body staining sand.

In warm pearl light of dawn next day the stripy tent is far away. A stopped clock propped proclaims a show at noon.

'No! Yes! No!' The voice persists inside his head. 'There is a man. I think he's dead.'

'It's now too late' his voices state. The strange stained words
are in his mouth. The strange strained voice is in his head.

On Southwold beach a man is dead and in a heart no feeling.

1777 — School for Scandal

The Bathing Hut Affair

One does indeed look at handsome young fishermen in a new light if one has been fortunate enough to see Mr Sheridans' new play on the London stage.

We travelled to Southwold in my uncle's new carriage. Taking the sea air had been prescribed on the grounds of my delicate health. I do indeed get pounding headaches when I become bored by endless needlework and shrill recitals. But I absolutely love the theatre. After seeing *School for Scandal* I purchased the dearest little dog and called it Scandal too! I thought it rather witty because I shall surely have to school it!

I had heard from my cousin that there were a number of bathing huts on Southwold beach, a racy prospect! It is whispered but not confirmed, that one descends into the water naked in order to get maximum exposure to sun and sea. I quite blush to think of it, but very diverting if true. Young Doctor Willis all but prescribed it during my last visit. His eyes tend to lower towards my neckline as he takes my pulse. I confess I do blush and my heart quite races during his visits.

Walking past the fishing boat men, I have to confess, I did see one that took my fancy. His bearing was that of one high born. Could it be that his patched smock is only the guise of poverty. Taking a lover from the lower orders is all the rage this summer, thanks to Mr Sheridan. I feigned interest in something far out to sea as I am sure he was looking in my direction as he mended his nets.

Was it my fancy that the wind whipped up when I saw him? Was the sun somewhat hotter as I felt my cheeks burn.

I know I became unbearably conscious of my slim ankles showing as my dress billowed out in the strongest gusts of summer breeze. I felt sure his rough but gentle eyes were following my innocent promenade. I must confess I felt all confusion.

My destination was to inspect the wheeled huts lined up against the low under cliff. Was one indeed shielded from public gaze as one descended into the waves?

Becky, my giddy young maid started to suppress a giggle, as did I, when a portly gentleman emerged, his nakedness only partially shielded by the low awning.

At last I see some bobbing heads of young ladies bathing at the far end of the beach. They seem to be quite enjoying their medicinal emersion.

I will perhaps venture in that direction tomorrow.

1849 — Mr Dickens Visits

'Thankee kindly Mr Dickens zir, thankee.' The young porter strutted away having pocketed a bright new sixpence and a tale to tell his friends.

'All aboard for Yarmouth,' the stationmaster called as he paced proudly along the platform whistle in hand. It was not every day that a well known literary gentleman frequented his station.

'All aboard!'

I closed the carriage door behind me in the hope of discouraging others from using it. I sat back in my plump first class seat.

Closing my eyes I drifted back in time. Faces from my childhood floated into my mind. Suddenly a leather case was held up to the window of my carriage with a call of 'Is this yours?'

I stood and looked up at the string luggage rack above my head — my case was not there.

'Why yes, Sir. By Jove it is!' I said opening the carriage door.

'Thought so!'

The young man fairly leapt into the carriage.

Moments later the guard blew his whistle. The train lurched and began to puff and heave itself out of the station.

'You left it in the tea shop and…by Jove aren't you…I mean you look very like a picture I saw… in a periodical… of a Mr Dick…' the young man stopped and looked quizzical.

'Mr Dickens. Yes — yes indeed I am.'

'David Copperforth at your service.'

We shook hands and sat down opposite one another in the smart modern railway carriage of 1849.

'Well, well, Sir. My good friend Steerfield will be exceedingly amazed that I have met you — exceedingly amazed! He greatly enjoys your work, Sir.'

I smiled at the excited young man who reminded me so much of my younger self and put the leather case on the seat beside me.

I was obviously in a forgetful frame of mind – not surprising, I thought to myself, as I was about to retrace some bittersweet childhood steps. Those last few happy days by the sea in Yarmouth and that last day in Southwold, before I was sent away into the darkness of my boyhood factory gloom.

'You must tell your friend how happy I am to hear of his enjoyment of my stories. And I certainly owe you a debt of gratitude, Sir. You saved a precious manuscript from being lost'

'Oh I am sure they would have put the case into the lost property for you at the station, Mr Dickens.'

'But that is far from certain. There are many about these days that might have appropriated such a leather case for profit.'

'It is certainly an unusual bag' replied the young man.'What a tale I will have to tell Steerfield!'

'I call it my writing bag. At present it contains the beginnings of a story as yet unnamed.' I patted the shiny leather and ran my thumb along the stitching.

'I got it during my last trip to the Americas," I continued. 'They are becoming quite popular in that great country. My barrister friend, Mr Wentworth, now uses one to carry around his chancery papers. He calls it his *briefcase* although his papers and discourse are far from brief!' I laughed.

'It is certainly a most unusual case, Mr Dickens,' exclaimed the young man. Perhaps it will catch on in the city'

*   *   *   *

I leant back and closed my eyes.

I had not much enjoyed my bumpy carriage ride from Halesworth to Southwold. But once there I strolled along the beach path and even took my shoes and socks off in memory of my childhood. Breathing in the salty sea air I felt more relaxed.

I had always looked on my day in Southwold as the last day of my freedom, before my shock when the jaws of London swallowed me up. No wonder Peggotty's eyes had been bright with tears. As a boy I had thought it was the wind.

After a jug of ale and a good portion of meat pie at the local hostelry I took a stroll down to the harbour to find a skiff that would take me somewhat more gently back along the Blyth to Halesworth.

The sun was quite low in the sky. I took out my pocket watch as I disembarked from the skiff. There was, as I had thought, just time to catch the connection to Yarmouth.

On arrival in Yarmouth I wrote for a short while then left the hotel for a summer's evening walk along harbour.

My eye caught sight of a weather beaten face of a sailor and a bright eyed young woman sitting together on the quay mending a fishing net.

There were a few dark clouds on the low horizon and a few seagulls flying inland.

'Look Em'ly see them gulls. I recon there will be storm tonight'

I stopped.

'A storm you say, is it certain?'

''Tis like as not sir — like as not.'

'We'll see it come in from home.'

'So you live close by?

'That's our house,' the old sailor indicated with his pipe and a twinkle in his eye.

There was a black upturned barge or ship not far off, high and dry on the rising ground adjacent to the shore. It had an iron funnel sticking out of its hull for a chimney and it was smoking very cosily.

After a little further talk about the fish that were to be found in the sea around Yarmouth, I walked on.

Walking back along the harbour, I encountered my new found acquaintance from the train. We stopped to admire the early evening harbour view.

'Don't you think that very remarkable sky?' Mr Copperforth said. 'I don't recall ever having seen one like it. I am waiting for my friend Steerfield's sailing ship to arrive from Spain. I do hope there will not be a storm.'

The skies were a murky confusion. Blotted with a colour like that of smoke from damp fuel. There had been a wind all day and it was rising with a strange low moaning sound.

I took my leave and offered the hope that if there was to be a storm it would pass quickly.

As the night advanced sweeping gusts of rain came up like curtains of steel. When the day broke the wind blew harder. In mighty gusts it was blowing dead on shore, its force became more and more terrific. I went down to look at the sea. Staggering along I became afraid of falling slates and tiles.

On the beach the boatmen and half the people of the town, were lurking behind buildings or braving the fury of the storm and then blown back. Joining these groups, I found women whose husbands were away in the herring boats. Old sailors shook their heads, as they looked from water to sky. Everyone was disturbed and anxious.

As the high watery walls came rolling in, they looked as if they would engulf the town. The receding waves seemed to scoop out deep caves in the beach, as if its purpose were to undermine the earth. Masses of water shivered and shook the beach with a booming sound.

Back at the hotel I tried to rest, but in vain, it was five o'clock in the afternoon. Later I sat by the coffee-room fire. The waiter told me he'd heard that, down the coast, two boats had gone down with all hands.

I hastily ordered my dinner. The wind was rising. The howl and roar, the rattled the doors and windows, rumbling in the chimneys. There was now a great darkness and unintelligible fear. I tried fitfully again to sleep.

Someone was knocking and calling at my door.

'What is the matter?' I cried.

'A wreck! Close by!'

I sprung out of bed, and asked, 'What wreck?'

'A schooner, from Spain. Make haste, Sir, if you want to see her! It's thought she'll go to pieces any moment.'

All were running in one direction to the beach. I ran the same way and soon came facing the wild sea.

I looked out to sea for the wreck and saw nothing but the foaming heads of the great waves.

A half-dressed boatman, standing next to me, pointed with his bare arm to the left. Then I saw it close into shore.

One mast was broken short off, six or eight feet from the deck, and lay over the side, entangled in a maze of sail and rigging.

112

A great cry, which was momentarily audible even above the wind, rose from the shore at this moment.

There was a bell on board. The ship rolled and dashed like a desperate creature driven mad, showing the whole sweep of her deck as she turned on her beam-ends towards the shore. The ship's bell tolled.

The wreck was breaking up. She was parting in the middle. The life of the solitary man hanging onto the mast hung by a thread. Still, he clung to it. Until there was a great rising wave. Then lost beneath the foam the ship was gone!

As I staggered through the gale, back to my hotel someway along the Yarmouth strand, I was greatly troubled. I had nowhere seen my newfound acquaintance Copperforth on the shore. Had I witnessed the demise of his friend Steerfield to a watery grave?

On gaining the shelter of my room I took up pen and paper and began to write of the events of such a fearful night.

The description of the storm in this story is largely taken from David Copperfield.

The tempest scene in David Copperfield is set at Yarmouth and is reputedly based on Dickens' own experiences when he stayed there in 1849. A Southwold detour seemed plausible. Part of the 1969 film David Copperfield *was shot on location in Southwold.*

The first modern rectangular briefcase is said to have been first made in the 1850s.

1872 — 'Lady' Adnams Summer Cup

Well, they called her 'Lady' Adnams on account of her sons taking over the brewery an' plastering their name across it. We was perfickly sure that were her idea. Though we never knew fer certain. 'T'was whispered her father maybe was a lord who payed fer her fancy education at Miss Potts'. Lovely airs and graces she 'ad — lovely as she walked home from school back in the day. I followed her down to the harbour when I saw her with her basket goin' down to get some early Friday fish. An' sometimes she'd look back an' giggle cos she knew that I were there. I were clear in love with her growin' up. Ma would catch me moonin' at her when I saw her 'bout the town.

When growed I took deliveries to her back door on times an' hung about to try to get a glimpse of her.

'Corse, as we all know, she married Adnams and I fer one will never know why. But out neighbour's girl Mary came along the road one day all growed up! An' she'd become ever so pretty an' I fell for her, an' she fer me.

We was soon married, happy as larks.

1872 that were when the Adnams took over the brewing in Southwold. Her boys were called Ernest an' George — an our boy Silas went finding birds nests with young George one time and scraped his knees. Ma said they were rough house boys and he weren't to go with them again for all their h'educated ways.

The Summer Cup was 'Lady' Adnams' idea for something fer the ladies to drink when they needed something more thirst quenching than gin or a small sup of tea.

They had a grand opening fer Adnams with free beer. An' they had bunting right the way down to the Nelson, with a brass band and such — as well as a charity bizarre in the Sailors' Reading Room. We all dressed up in our Sundays even though it were Saturday.

The new, much advertised Summer Cup, was in a big silver bowl with silver ladles an' all, with chopped strawberries and mint an' such like floating in the bowl. Me wife's cup looked right pretty with them bits of fruit in — an' she said it wer' good stuff. Sweet Beer she said it were. Ladled out, it was, by 'Lady' Adnams herself — in an h'enormous hat. Bootiful she looked, bootiful. Me wife had a twinkle in her eye after a sip or two. Silas an' I had normal brew.

The Summer Cup were so popular they brought it out every summer fer the ladies to have in the snug or in the little garden out back.

That William Morris from London made Southwold quite famous ten year before with his poem an' such. So more visitors came from up London Town than ever before to take the air. We heard Doctors prescribed the air fer health an' such like. The railway came in a few years later.

An' Lady Adnams cut the red ribbon to open the station 1879. That were a day but no free beer that time. An' Lady Adnams Summer Cup were on sale too fer thruppence and in a bottle! We all called her 'Lady Thruppence' after that!

1893 — Miss Prism Retires

I always was forgetful – even as a young girl I would forget the time. I remember nanny on Southwold beach with her watch resting on her large round bosom. 'Time waits for no one' she would say staring out to sea. She had what she called 'regrets'. She was kind sometimes, I remember. She wore a cherry hat on Sundays in St Edmunds church with the fierce angels that peered over their piers looking down on us with their long noses.

Mostly it was a happy childhood but I remember crying myself to sleep one night. I was seven years old. I remember because no one could come to my seventh birthday party because I had a dreadful cold. Mother and my sister Griselda brought my birthday tea up on a tray and there was my very first little bear sitting up in bed with me. My only guest!

A week later, when I was better, I took my bear into the wood behind our house. Griselda was at school and I was allowed to wander on that sunny afternoon as long as I could see the house. So we picked bluebells – Bear-Bear and I. I sat him on a log, as I went to pick them. Our garden robin came to watch me too in the afternoon sunshine. I had my crumpled hanky in my pocket in case I sneezed. It was the one I had embroidered with my initials in chain stitch. With my large bunch of bluebells I followed our robin back into our garden and found a pot to put them in. I was allowed to put them on the tea table but I remember feeling sad because they drooped so quickly.

I got out my paint box after tea, trying to capture the beautiful cascading blue. Griselda said she loved the painting and we

117

put it up on the mantle shelf. She married an army officer and went away to India – he was very dashing with a huge moustache that drooped quite as much as the bluebells did when they were picked.

I only remembered Bear-Bear when I got into bed without him. I asked Mama if I could go and get him but it was too late and I wasn't allowed to go. A few minutes after I blew out the candle — feeling rather lonely without my Bear-Bear. The wind started howling round the house and a few minutes after that I heard the rain drops beating on the window pane. I thought of poor Bear-Bear out there in the wood all alone in a rain storm due to my forgetfulness. It made me feel lonely to think of it and tears trickled down my cheek until my pillow was quite wet. The wetness of my pillow quite surprised me and I wondered if Bear-Bear would get blown away as well as sodden. I thought perhaps I would never find him again.

After breakfast I begged Mama to let me go quickly to find him but it was still raining. As I was just getting better from the cold that had kept me off school all week, I simply wasn't allowed to go out until the rain had stopped. I waited all morning, watching the raindrops sliding down the window pane, promising myself and God that I would never ever forget anything ever ever again.

I was allowed to go out in my mackintosh and galoshes after lunch and found him in the bluebells behind the log. Something must have nibbled him in the night because he had a horrible hole in his tummy and his some of his stuffing had fallen out and he was so very wet! I tried to squeeze him dry but he just kept on dripping!

I was mortified and cried again. My beautiful Birthday Bear-Bear looked old and bedraggled. He had certainly been in the wars. Mama helped me mend him but he never ever looked smart again. His stitched tummy and funny smell, even after he had dried out, always reminded me of my forgetfulness. And somehow I still forget things and muddle things up especially when I am in a hurry.

That's how the baby was left on the train and the manuscript put in the perambulator when I was a governess for the Bracknells in London.

I had been writing my manuscript of a romantic novel as the baby slept on the way to Brighton. Sea air is so good for babies you know. Then when the railway conductor came I just couldn't find my ticket and in all the kerfuffle the baby was forgotten. There was such a to-do – such a dreadful thing to do. How could I return to the family residence without it – the baby, — I mean.

I later got 12 guineas for the novel when it was published but I could never write another – not after loosing the baby. He was from such a good family too. His father was a general. In fact, now I come to think of it, the General had such pop-out staring eyes. I'm quite sure his eyes bore a remarkable likeness to Bear-Bear and if I remember correctly, which sadly is not always the case, there was a rumour in the household that the General had a war wound too — just like my bear. So you see, I just couldn't go back. I just went away and life went on, and after some time I forgot.

It was a very great relief when it all came out.

Lady Bracknell frightened the life out of me when she pronounced 'Prism' in her imperious voice after all those years. It is a voice one could hardly forget, even if one is forgetful.

The Bracknells were somewhat forgiving. I was able, after Cecily got married, to retire to my Southwold family home. Dear Dr. Chasuble helps out in the church services and we pass many a pleasant afternoon on the promenade talking of old times, although of course much has been forgotten. I will not, however, travel on the Southwold Line. I cannot now be persuaded to board any train after that terrible kerfuffle due to my forgetful nature.

As nanny said all those years ago I have 'regrets'.

Mrs Wilde was most sympathetic when I told her my story. We had struck up a friendship when she was taking the air at Southwold for medicinal purposes. Her boys love flying their kite on Southwold beach. Of course I didn't know then she was *the* Mrs Wilde. To me she was a slightly frail young mother who I invited to tea in my dear little house.

I let her boys play with Bear-Bear and told them he was a general with staring eyes, who had an old war wound.

Mrs Wilde invited me to come to London to see her husband's new play, *The Importance of being...* someone or other — I forget. But I felt the journey to London to be overlong for me these days. As of course I can no longer bring myself to travel by train after that dreadful todo, all those years ago, on the Brighton Line.

1969 — Southwold Bovver

Well I told her it was an unmentionable subject. But she would go on…

I kept on knitting right through the 'ole thing. I kept on casting on new colours, pretending I wasn't listening but I was. 'course I was – couldn't help it.

The scarf's turned out quite different now from how I meant it. I couldn't give it to Charlie now. Not now there's so much in it. Too many colours. Too much of what she was telling me, I s'pose.

No, it'll have to go to them refugees now. I told her there's too many colours in it now.

'I used to like colours,' she said. 'Used to like seeing bright sky on Sunday a'ternoons and yellow buttercups that told you if you liked butter.'

Charlie goes out on Sundays. Well he goes out most days. He doesn't know I sit next to her at the centre sometimes. He wouldn't approve if he knew.

I know she didn't do right but when I think what happened to her — what they did, that wasn't right neither. Mind you what she did wasn't right for all she says: 'I did it for love, Luv'.

That's what she says on the days when she does talk, which ain't many. Most days she stares into space. I think she's got to have an operation on her eyes soon. I reckon her room's draughty. That's what does it. Her eyes keep on watering.

Charlie would probably belt her one if he saw her wet face. He'd think she was crying. 'Not here, not now' he'd say in his tightest voice. Not even moving his lips almost. He'd make a good ventriloquist, would our Charlie. He can speak without moving a muscle. It's true.

The statue of Our Lady speaks like that too sometimes when I go to the Catholic Church which isn't as often as I should. I should confess every time I go, but I don't.

Charlie doesn't like it — me going to the church. He says it's all my fault for being so stupid — which is true. 'Specially when things get difficult, I get stupid. Then I have to clean up the mess when he throws his dinner across the room. 'cause I've done it wrong because I'm stupid. So stupid I am.

Sorry Charlie, I'll say.

Stupid cow, he'll say.

Shall I do you some more, Charlie, I'll say.

Do it right he'll say.

All without moving his lips. It's amazing.

Yes… he'd belt her if he saw her, belt her for looking stupid on her off days. And for talking too much when someone listens.

Our Lady listens to me when the Church is open. There's a seat in the porch if it's locked. Even if I have to sit out side, I know she hears me. But it does get perishing cold, even though you're out of the wind.

Mind you, he'll always have me back. However mad I make him, he always lets me cook his breakfast. He'll joke then and say: 'You were gone a long time, were you with your toy boy?'

'You wouldn't let me in Charlie. You locked the door and bolted it.'

'Did I?' He'll say. 'I don't remember.'

He don't remember much. So he'll always have me back.

She don't remember much either.

The thing that gets me is… that she always wears dirty ankle socks and shoes that don't fit her. I suggest she wear dark glasses to hide her eyes but she says 'what for?' And I didn't like to tell her.

Well of course she don't know what her eyes look like, straggling in different directions. Very off putting it is… very.

They look as if …they're looking everywhere. But she don't see nothing at all, not ever nowadays.

And it's not my job to do up the zip on her dress is it?

And I don't think anyone could get a comb through her hair if they tried.

She used to be such a pretty kid.

The voices tell me her husband wants to tell me something. But I don't know if they're wrong or right.

I never know.

The voices tease me sometimes and tell me things that just aren't true. Sometimes they tell me bad things about Charlie. And I tell 'em off then, 'cause Charlie's a good man. He just needs a drink now and again to keep things *even-Stephen*, if you know what I mean – medicinal. And he gets lots of money when he takes back all the bottles — loads.

You should see the bins when his mates come by.

Charlie's got lots of mates — loads. And they all go off to football matches and rallies in coaches.

True Brits, that's what they are. Flying the flag. And they tell all the people from India and Africa, they can go back there. Not that there's any round here of course.

But Charlie says he could get a job if they went back.

That's what gets him mad about her. She married one of them. Had his children.

'Disgusting!' Charlie said and worse. Sometimes he would shout 'Rivers of blood' out the window 'cause of that Enoch Powell man.

Charlie was questioned about it. They kept him in the Nick for several days questioning him about whether he was in the area... 'course I said he was with me. They wanted to see his clothes. But we'd had a bonfire out the back and burned loads of stuff with his mates.

And everyone thinks she shouldn't have married him 'cause he was from Africa. Anyway, seeing them together upset people... him being ever so tall and black as night. Charlie said something had to be done about it.

Nobody liked it.

And all them kids... was disgusting.

Charlie couldn't stand it. He worked himself up about it.

He was always weight training, every night.

He's quite short is our Charlie but he's ever so strong.

She's short too. They made a lovely couple growing up. Everyone said so.

Childhood sweethearts they were.

Charlie was always the jealous type. He used to keep her close – out of harms way like.

Perhaps he should have taken her out a bit more. But they wanted to save for a house so bad.

Then before you could say 'Jack Robinson,' she'd got married behind his back.

Charlie was so mad. But he didn't say nothing. Not for years. But I knew. I may be stupid, but I knew he weren't right. He walked a bit tighter and started putting out flags

Mind you, I like our Union Jacks. But they're quite big and the neighbours complain about them hanging out the windows all the time. He even has one tattooed on his forehead, and somewhere else, where he won't tell me. Which he never regretted… because he was always telling me that.

Mind you I always thought he walked a bit funny after… sort of bow-legged. I've got used to the one on his forehead… sort of. But I don't really like it as much as he does. But he doesn't have to look at it all the time and… I think the tattooist must have probably had had one too many, 'cause it's not on quite straight.

They say tattooing hurts a lot.

And she hurts a lot too… 'cause of her eyes and 'cause they all died in the fire, all except her. They found her tied to a chair by the bonfire with her eyes all punched to bits and she didn't know who it was what done it. She don't remember so they was never caught. Charlie says he's sorry but she shouldn't have gone messing about. She remembered something the other day, that's what she was telling me... About when she was little and she and Charlie used to play together. That was what she was saying, about their games and how they used to play 'blindfold and kidnap' and 'mothers and fathers'.

'I don't want to know that stuff,' I said. But she would keep on about it. Telling me details like. Charlie was a naughty boy in those days.

I had no idea. I just kept on listening and knitting.

And I thought to myself: 'It's a good job our Charlie has mended his ways.'

2020 — Southwold Gulls

Writers sometimes see the future. Daphne du Maurier certainly did. She lived by the sea and had experienced the eyes of gulls — their bullying and determined ways — their propensity to cluster around the munching tourist trade. She saw how they scrapped over scraps, gliding with levels of demented concentration — focus that bordered on addiction.

Slavering dogs in a medieval court do not match them. These winged pack hunters are clannish and cold, fierce as the salt whipped winds from the Arctic. Soft fat fleshed and TV blanched the vacuous visitors filled faces and fattened rounded stomachs to pocket pulling proportions.

Gulls wing-watched the weaving sun baked Saturday streets. It was a star-spangled summer celebration, through holiday heat-waving crowds. In a pulsating US style parade, though strongly opposed by the locals, MacD's Burgers had come to town.

On the Fifth of July in Southwold something snapped.

Fire cracking Fourth of July fireworks had disturbed their evening. Gulls wheeled and whirled over the salt licked town screeching harshly to each other throughout the night. Like disgruntled fishwives they cursed on the wing, swirling through the darkness like angry angels.

As above so below.

Wakeful tourists tossed in their beds. Sweating their bulging burgered, bulk in squeaking beds. Kids kicked at cot bars sulkily screaming for pop, for crisps, to play Nintendo. Teens and twenty-somethings turned on or zoned out, as the starlit sky was churned by a wheeling fractal frenzy of sea-gulled shadows swirling.

Disturbing.

At high noon the local Concrite twins, next-fix needy, emerged predatorily from their 'Crow's Nest' flat perched high above the streets. Sunglassed, gummed and identically earpodded, the twins swaggered slowly seaward. The hated sun glare penetrated spiked skulls. Bedevilled brains and opportunity were very soon lightly fingering their sweating collars.

The open door an invitation. The bag on the table open. One looked over — one looked out. Cold eyes casing. The overripe purse was ready for plucking. A hard hand pinch-pecked and pocket swallowed. Their fast footsteps flew towards some shadowed safety. Entrails spilled — cards, coins, crumpled notes.

The predatory pair picked over contents. The dry fish stink merged with sweat and something more enticing. Something more mouth watering was nudging their Concrite nostrils. An arresting aroma came curvaceously curling into Concrite consciousness — MacDominANT Burgers and Fries.

Crouching bodies straightened. Mesmerised, the twins turned towards town. Urgent in their need for their fast food fix of MacD's delicious delights. Craving caught and cussed, oily with sun sweated skin and ripening red necked pimples. Drawn like two magnetised pins, like dogs they followed the scent.

MacDominANT's smiling Demon Ant logo beckoned with bright red plasticity. With smell of deeply dreamed hypnotically honed fiendish flavours of fantasy fries. Mingling erotically with big bunned burgers

Devilicious!

MacDominANT's ant horns visually echoed the plastic ant's sickly smile. Each bag topped with a long fry, curved on top in the upturned horn/smile shape. Children ate the smile or devil horn depending on mood.

It was a benediction of sorts. A ritual eating of flesh and fries and red pop effervescent blood. Little devils sick of sin, slurping sticky red slush from round rimmed cups. The thin red pop smile stain extended logo-ed lips — smile-stamped. Smugly they sauntered, fat bagged and harbour-wards, in Sunday step towards the gulls.

Bits of buns and burgers were greedily gobbled.

Gaunt gimlet gull eyes wing watched twixt earth and heaven. They did not fall as angels sometimes do. One wing-folded. Diving so suddenly — so deeply at the prey that others followed fiercely, disturbing the sea-slapped air. Disturbing pensioners at prayer. With irreverent clownish squawking, they self-served with swerving swoop.

Screaming — screaming — screaming. They took the burger bread. Take, eat — this is my body. They spilled the popping effervescent blood. They took the cup — worshipping the craving image the Red Ant Christ.

They came in droves. Breathless little children.

Stuff, suffer, stuff. Puff, puffer, puff.

Little children getting larger, getting more of what they wanted, getting the fast food fix. So were the gull. Addiction is careless of consequence. So are gulls

At first a fat-fleshed fingered fist fought for custody of a half torn bag of fries and smiling devil's horn. But torn fleshed iron smell of blood stimulated further feasting and flocking, stirring sky.

Fathers fought feathered gull addicts. Strong single fathers – out for the day suddenly doing what fathers should. Fighting for family, protecting progeny. Mothers swarmed into shops dragging bedraggled screamers, until the glass shattered…

Dogs that have tasted blood can never again be trusted with sheep or lamb of God.

Guttural blood thirsty gulls gorged on fattened burgered flesh. Gulls' first choice now…

Over the wide world seagulls scanned for well oiled skin, containing burger fried fat, converted into human flesh that first spilled out on Southwold pavements. The culling had begun. The war of worlds, of those above and those below and who will win?

The gods will know.

Phosphorescence

This is a night of nights, a night to imagine, a night to truly live. This night of wondrous real-world magic cast a spell. There is an escapade afoot!

The two of us, dressed in velvet darkness, ascend the dunes. Sometimes we falter before our eyes adjust to the light of stars. A dark panorama unfolds before us. Far out to sea distant cargos of light await the day. Sparkling strangely the stars blink on and off in low horizon over the slowly stirring molasses sea. Whilst high above the beach the star dome slowly wheels its stately dance in perfect step with time.

And yet we see the lower sky above the sea is host to a myriad of winking stars. We wonder at the magic cause of this. Searching for our ancient glowing treasure quest we stumble along the darkly heaving waters edge and hear the suck and thrust of breathing waves. Giggling like girls we see white starlit foam — spit flow from Neptune's body.

We walk the sandbar darkness searching for the phosphorescent sea, scanning dark water for natural magic lighting up the waves. Walking under a fisherman's line we wonder. Maybe this is not the night.

At last we have ignition and see a gently sparking wave of luminescence. It is an eerie light inside the rolling foam and then another lighting up the rolling tumble as it comes restlessly reaching towards the shore.

Now we see we see the game, as the rippling all along the wave length light is flaring! The dark sea surface further out is all alight now. The tarry water is lit with sparkling sea stars echoing the meteor shower above. The sea it seems is lighting up for us. It seems to know our game and wants to play!

We long to be enfolded in this magical event.

Quickly naked we wade into the waves. Each move we make up-lights the waves with strange cold fire that is entrancing. We are dancing, churning tarry darkness into light. We are the children of an August night. Now we become magical beings that can light up the waves and water as it swirls around us.

In this symphony of sea and stars. We play a movement. We are the alchemy between dark water and the phosphorescent light. It seems we are unfolding time backwards as we are reborn.

Now we are magical beings manifesting light within the waves — as if this light was hidden till we came. Gently immersed in this womb of dark water infused with light we become baptised. In this deluge of natural wonders we are deeply surrendered to joy. We revel in the wonder and the sheer delight of swimming in this phosphorescent night.

Black Shuck

A Suffolk Legend of Beccles, Blythburgh and Southwold

Hell had opened its gaping mouth of black storm and coated the sky. Hairs rose on man and dog alike.The air had trembled in the heat of that long afternoon.

Suddenly a fireball cracked — a deafening roar that broke the steeple. Stopping time itself. It broke time in pieces, hands and all.

Hail drove harsh ice knives into smoking thatch and steeple, and into flesh as people ran from that sky-born hound of hell. They ran from screaming streaming eye of storm into the sanctified house and prayed. They prayed for deliverance and tried to sing a thunder punctuated hymn. But it has to be said they were all sinners.

Then the great door blew agape. The growling maelstrom came marauding into church with the roaring wind and rain. Caught in lightening spotlight — a hellish silhouette. With one great howl, a giant dog stood beside the font. Then an answering human howl as a body was dragged into the aisle. A throat torn open — blood, flesh and rolling eyes caused screams of pain.

A ripping of flesh as lightening tore the sky. The scream of howling wind commingled with a congregation's moans of fear. The stench of a great wet pelt of dog - the iron smell of pooling, dripping blood filled the air. Then the dog was gone.

The devil ran 12 miles with dripping mouth and paws and claws and bloodied coat. With raging breath it clawed the great closed doors of Blythburgh church, then turned away. The great brute killed and maimed the ale wives' drunken men who had not gone to church. So they were burned by devilled breath that made a Suffolk legend.

Running on to Southwold streets towards the dawn, it tossed a rat for pleasure. Some said there was a baby gone, a child that's lost forever. It was a Devil Dog for sure. They say it sailed away from shore and was last seen aboard a Flanders-bound.

A Devil beast, that bloodied hound, but never more its like was found. It left a tale for us to tell, of bloodied Black Shuck — dog from hell.

Striding out on Southwold Pier

Stride out on the pier in winter wrapped up warm and armed with this poem!

Striding its sturdy columns defiantly out

into the — sometimes vicious — cold North Sea

It will not — we hope — set sail.

Taking a deep breath to walk its length

and down a coffee — off we set

determined strides

counter the bullying punching gusts.

We are the winter warmer girls

coat wrapped — pull hatted

scarf knotted — winter booted

warm trousered — thermal vested

woollen socked — sturdy knickered

hands pocketed — gloves mislaid

as we stride out — high winds and life elicit tears

and pound white waves beneath

the swirling sea is seen in spaces

through slightly shaking board walk planks

ruffling the pent up surge that thunders underfoot

What was that you said — I said — oh never mind — what?
words of wisdom lost and tossed by wild uncaring wind
our words are wind-whipped out of earshot
over the ice cold rail into a broiling sea
seated in a cold Tim Hunkin's metal booth
we get more swirling air — rugs and warming drinks
tasting salt lips — hands shelter hot bitter
shall I sugar it? — coffee foam
hair whips into mouths as well as coffee
oh lets go inside — what?

The clock-house back door slams
sheltered now we wonder aloud
about the possibility of cake
sweet mouthed we watch white horses thunder in
there is no other show in town — I've got to go
and so must I — a chorus party piece
of sugared speak
so
coat wrapping —pull hatting
scarf knotting — winter booting
warm trousering — thermal vesting

woollen stocking — sturdy knickers

deeply shocking

hand pocketed — gloves mislaid

door banging — determined striding

countering — gusting

bullying — punching

wild winds thrusting

while winter walking

on Southwold Pier.

Doggerlands and Shifting Sands

10,000 years ago

Speculate upon a long lost land. A kingdom there was, perhaps, but now without a king or queen or kitchen maid.

From these long lost deep drowned lands old dripping bones are sometimes dredged. Deck dried on the cold sea swell. It's well known us fisherfolk have tales to tell.

We net this long lost land along with our fish. It's long drowned worlds build fractured pictures of an ancient people living out their days.

Animals there were to tend and meadows too, wind blown with nodding flower heads and corn. They heard the birds call out with each new dawn.

Sea raised a water wall that drowned the Dogger people — overwhelming ways of life that filled their days and nights, when eye bright fire confabulated tales.

Ancient Dogger people your long lost lands are fathoms deep in time — marinated in the brine.

High seas are rising now — as then they rose, breaking over heads as waves sweep in and swallow living heat as cold eyes close, sending souls swirling, stiffening, curling round rocks down deep under shoals. Below the rocking waves where cradled children sleep. Slowly silting into mud and sand.

What once were sunlit rolling lands are sown with seaweed, swaying darkly under the North Sea drift. A long forgotten people's vibrant life is now reduced to dripping bones dredged up and roughly torn from ancient soft sand beds of rest.

There are no voices left to cry 'do not disturb'. Their bones, in sunlight, left left to dry. Only swaying sailors' ropes sing out in the wind sheer scream. Gulls cry like mourners trailing ships to shore.

Speculate on our own long drowned demise, in some far futured scene. With dark waves rolling deep above our long lost lands, our bones are dredged. Museum catalogued in drawers.

Then play a thought of what there might have been. A kingdom here — perhaps with king or queen and kitchen maid.

It may be so — but now such memories are long lost, swirling into Ozimandias's sand, now fathoms deep. His once proud stare, and curling sneer are legacy to our profligate and careless lives.

JayJay Hunter Dunn in Southwold

inspired by John Betjeman

JayJay Hunter Dunn — oh! Jay you're such fun
as we set off to Southwold — for our morning run
three miles or five miles — a wonderful jog
when you are beside me — it's never a slog.

Each day when we meet — it is such breathless fun
I just love to text you — I know you're the 'One'
Each morning we drink down our green herbal tea,
how healthy life is now — when you swim with me!

You were wonderfully pictured — in our local press,
A marathon winner — I'm in love, I confess
On the floor of your bedroom, my singlet and shorts,
And your cream-coloured room is be-trophied with sports.

Facebook and Instagram now need updating
we must not keep social media waiting
As we text in your courtyard — we sip Suffolk gin
the bubbling Jacuzzi entices us in.

Through your organic garden — together we walk,
we kiss by your raised beds — holding hands as we talk
The Tesla is waiting — we drive to the sea
All's right with the world, Jay — when you drive with me.

Again off to Southwold — our place on the coast
a friend of ours' party — he's such a good host
we kiss and we smile — holding each others gaze
as we sip Adnam's Fizz — we are in quite a daze.

We sail up the Blyth in the last of the light
and listen to owl hoots long into the night
The full moon is rising —a bat flies about
'Lets have a night swim' — we hear someone shout.

Naked we splash out in dark velvet waves
everyone's laughing and no-one behaves
we party all night till the rise of the sun
I'm so glad I *Tindered* you Jay Hunter Dunn

Caroline Gay Way